"We both want to make this transition work."

Rio slowly nodded, as if not yet convinced. "I guess it wouldn't hurt. Maybe we can try it tomorrow, anyway."

"That's all I ask."

Her mouth curved. "Not asking much, are you?"

With a sense of elation that he'd won her over, Cash couldn't help but share her smile as they openly studied each other, her mind likely teeming with as many questions about their working relationship as filled his. If he guessed right, this spunky lady kept many a man on his toes these days, and not because they were on guard for an ambush as he'd often been in his youth.

Looking down at her, he caught the soft, quick intake of her breath before she abruptly spun away and started down the trail back to the heart of the Hideaway.

"See you at sunrise," she called over her shoulder with a sassy toss of that ponytail, and he shook his head. This might prove to be a long—and interesting—few months.

Glynna Kaye treasures memories of growing up in small Midwestern towns—and vacations spent with the Texan side of the family. She traces her love of storytelling to the times a houseful of great-aunts and great-uncles gathered with her grandma to share candid, heartwarming, poignant and often humorous tales of their youth and young adulthood. Glynna now lives in Arizona, where she enjoys gardening, photography and the great outdoors.

Mountain Country Cowboy

Glynna Kaye

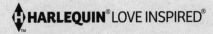

Recycling programs
for this product may
not exist in your area.

LOVE INSPIRED BOOKS

ISBN-13: 978-0-373-62305-1

Mountain Country Cowboy

www.Harlequin.com

Printed in U.S.A.

"For I know the plans I have for you," declares the Lord, "plans to prosper you and not to harm you, plans to give you hope and a future."
—*Jeremiah* 29:11

For it is by grace you have been saved, through faith—and this is not from yourselves, it is the gift of God—not by works, so that no one can boast.
—*Ephesians* 2:8–9

To my "Seeker Sisters"
at seekerville.blogspot.com.

Thank you for over a decade of love,
prayers and encouragement.

God did a beautiful thing
when He brought us together.

Mary Connealy

Janet Dean

Debby Giusti

Audra Harders

Ruth Logan Herne

Pam Hillman

Cara Lynn James

Myra Johnson

Sandra Leesmith

Julie Lessman

Tina Radcliffe

Missy Tippens

Chapter One

"Nice try, Grady, but I'm not buying it."

Riona "Rio" Hunter confidently shook her head as her older brother pulled a weathered suitcase out of her pickup truck and set it in the gravel at her booted feet. She gave him a serenely sweet smile, knowing his idea of welcoming her back to mountain country Arizona after a week's absence at a spiritual retreat would be to try to get her riled. "Grandma Jo wouldn't do something like that behind my back."

And certainly not right when they'd gotten word of a potential opportunity for a much-needed financial boost. Tallington Associates, an events coordinating company, would soon be evaluating the family-run Hunter's Hideaway that catered to outdoor enthusiasts as a possible recommended site for client gatherings. If all went as hoped, that contractor could be arranging bookings for years to come.

Grady shrugged. "Well, Grandma *did* do it. Like I said, Cashton Herrera interviewed several days ago, an offer was made and he'll be back to sign on the dotted line sometime today."

No way. She stared up at him. Was he telling the

truth? Both he and their other brother, Luke, were masters at keeping a straight face when they wanted to. Although Rio had plans to leave the family business later that summer and return to college, Grandma wouldn't hire someone without consulting her, would she? Rio's reservation for the out-of-state getaway had been made months ago, and Grandma couldn't wait one week for her to return?

Narrowing her eyes, she gave Grady a good-humored push. "Liar."

With a laugh, he reached out to playfully tug on the ponytail draped over her shoulder. "I'm not lying, Rio. It's a done deal. Ask her. Ask Mom and Dad. Cash arrives today to start as your assistant, then will step into full responsibility when you take off in August."

He *was* serious.

Grandma Jo hired a man—who not only had a reputation like that of his father for settling scores with his fists, but had even done jail time for striking a woman—to work with Rio?

"So you're telling me none of you voiced objections or bothered to call me so I could voice mine?" A pang of betrayal echoed in her heart. Knowing what they did regarding her past—and her intentions for the future—how could they be so insensitive? "You all know how I feel about men who hit."

They weren't *real* men.

Grady frowned, undoubtedly reminded of the distressing events at the conclusion of her freshman year at college. "Cash didn't try to hide his county jail record on the application form. And you already know Grandma followed up with his references, including a deputy sheriff who's been mentoring Cash for over three years and who personally doesn't believe he hit his ex-wife."

"But a *judge and jury* did believe it." With a huff, Rio grabbed the handle of her wheeled suitcase, dragging it toward the porch steps of her parents' cabin where, at twenty-one, she still resided. But not much longer, God willing.

Grady, swiftly blocking her way, reached down and relieved her of her luggage. "Come on now, calm down. You know Grandma Jo did this because she loves you and wants to give you the opportunity to chase your high-flying dreams."

He made it sound as if they were a passing fancy with no more substance than a soap bubble. As if she were a cute kitten fruitlessly attempting to pounce on a flitting butterfly and would soon tire and lose interest.

"But why did Grandma have to do interviews while I was out of town? And despite our looking at several promising applications, she picked a man like Cash?" Rio jerked her suitcase away from her brother, suspecting Grandma Jo had her eye on Cash all along and moved swiftly to hire him while her granddaughter was absent.

"He has an impressive background with horses, as well as dude ranch experience. And he aced the interview."

"But we both know," she almost growled, "that Grandma has a rescuer complex. She's big on second chances."

That's why she'd hired Cash's father those many years ago, wasn't it? And look how that turned out.

Rio abruptly shoved her suitcase back in her brother's direction. "Here, please take this and my other stuff inside. Tell Mom I won't be gone long, but I have to talk to Grandma."

"You're too late." He had the nerve to smile. Clearly she'd lost the ally she thought she'd have in Grady.

"We'll see about that."

Ignoring his chuckle, she spun on her booted heel and headed for a shortcut through the tall-trunked ponderosa pines leading to the Hideaway's main complex.

Cashton Herrera, of all people. As a skinny, dark-eyed boy six years her senior, he'd found it amusing to lock her in a utility closet when she was four years old—and that was just the beginning of his mischief at her expense. She was willing to concede that boys could be boys and grow up to be decent men. But jail time, well, that was an entirely different matter.

Up ahead through the trees she glimpsed the adjoining buildings that composed the heart of Hunter Enterprises—Hunter's Hideaway. A family business for six generations if you included the offspring of her four siblings, Hunter's Hideaway catered to hunters, horsemen, hikers and others who enjoyed spending time in the great outdoors.

Located not too far outside small-town Hunter Ridge, the property featured an inn, restaurant and general store. Guest cabins were scattered throughout a vast acreage that abutted National Forest Service property, and it was here that in addition to clerking, waiting tables and cleaning guest rooms, Rio managed seasonal trail and hay rides with assistance from a cousin and summer hires. But her cousin J.C., who she'd been counting on to take over for her when she headed back to college, had dashed off to chase his own rainbows.

So she was stuck here unless Cash proved capable of taking over her responsibilities. But even if he had the know-how to run the operation, how could she leave a man like him totally in charge? Hot tempers and ready fists wouldn't mix well with horses, guests or staff. Knowing how she'd feel about the new hire, was this a ploy on Grandma's part to keep her granddaughter from leaving?

As she stepped out from under the thick canopy of pine branches into a cloudless midmorning of the third week in May, she glimpsed a county sheriff's department SUV off to the side of the parking lot. And gritted her teeth.

Deputy Braxton Turner leaned casually against the vehicle, shooting the breeze with her older brother Luke. Which tattletale told Brax she'd arrive home today? It wasn't that she didn't like him. He was a nice enough guy—the attention he focused on her not nearly as irksome as that of Jeb Greer's son, Eliot, who'd recently returned for the summer—but she felt no sparks when in the company of either man. Nor did she, despite her best efforts, find trusting males outside the family an easy thing to do.

Besides, could neither of them see she had no intention of being trapped in a relationship that chained her to Hunter Ridge? She had a dream of helping others who, like herself, were victims of college dating violence. The last time she looked, though, tiny Hunter Ridge boasted no sprawling campus of higher learning where she could attain the needed counseling degree.

With a hasty wave in the direction of the two men, she dashed across the graveled parking lot, slowing to catch her breath when she reached the front porch entrance of the building that housed the inn and restaurant, as well as her grandmother's apartment and office.

She smoothed her shirt, somewhat wrinkled from the

California flight and a three-hour drive from Phoenix's Sky Harbor airport. It had been an emotionally, physically and mentally exhausting retreat focused on spiritual preparation for those intending to minister in the area of dating and domestic violence. Not only had she learned more about the spiritual aspects of how to reach out to victims of dating violence, but she'd been pressed to prayerfully dig deep down inside and relive her own experiences and further confront her fears. Every minute would be worth it, though, if she could apply what she'd learned to helping others in the future, the first step being when she returned to college in the fall— keeping the vow she'd made to God in exchange for His saving her mother's life after her cancer diagnosis.

With a silent, heartfelt prayer that she could convincingly express her concerns regarding Cash to Grandma Jo—and that she wasn't too late—she pulled open the heavy wood door. But she was immediately forced back as a ball-capped boy of seven or eight pushed out past her.

"Joseph!" a male voice bellowed from inside. "Get back here."

She peered into the dimly lit interior where a solidly built, broad-shouldered man rapidly approached from across the lobby. Dressed in dark jeans and a burgundy shirt, his head of jet-black hair topped by a Western hat, the grim set of his mouth clearly spelled out his exasperation.

Suddenly aware of someone holding open the door from which the child had bolted, the man paused, then touched the brim of his hat in acknowledgment. Midnight-dark eyes met hers with an unmistakable flicker of male interest, and her own betraying heart leaped in response to the approving appraisal. But his expression shuttered as he briskly nodded in the direction the escapee had taken.

"Pardon me, ma'am. I have a young'un to round up."

He obviously didn't recognize her after fourteen years. But she had no doubt as to *his* identity—and that she was too late to prevent Cashton Herrera from signing on at the Hideaway.

Cash couldn't lose a single second in pursuing his son, but for some reason his booted feet remained glued to the floor as he looked down at the petite young woman.

She gazed up at him as if in recognition, but while he might not be in the market for a lady these days— he'd learned his lesson the hard way with a cheating ex-wife—he'd not likely have forgotten that long, sun- streaked blond hair scooped high in a cascading pony- tail. Or the slightly crooked nose, sparkling blue eyes, and trim figure tucked into jeans and a light blue, fitted chambray shirt. Ear studs glimmered with silver and turquoise, a match to the Southwestern-styled watch gracing her wrist.

"So that was your boy, was it, who shot out of here like his pants were on fire?" Her voice was firm, di- rect. Like she knew him and was calling him out for an offense.

He'd sired Joseph Cashton Herrera when, at eigh- teen, he'd gotten involved with and married a pretty— and highly unpredictable—young woman. But the past forty-eight hours had been his first attempt at full-time, hands-on single parenting. As much as he'd dreamed of more time with his son, he hadn't been given any warn- ing that his ex would abruptly relinquish the child they shared. No time to prepare.

As a result, things weren't going all that well.

"Yeah, Joey's mine." Had the youngster gotten himself into trouble and fled the scene while his beleaguered daddy was filling out employment forms that would keep a roof over their heads? Cash squinted one eye. "Why do you want to know?"

A tiny crease formed between the woman's dark slash of brows. "No reason. Except I'm not surprised that a child of yours appears to be a handful. Kind of amusing, actually. What goes around comes around?"

He frowned. "Do we—"

"Rio! You're back."

Rio?

He turned to where his new employer, Josephine "Jo" Hunter, descended the staircase into the rustic inn and restaurant's lobby, her hair swept atop her head and secured with combs as he remembered she'd always worn it. Somewhere around eighty, she nevertheless donned jeans and a collared shirt and carried herself as regally as she had during the three years Cash's dad worked at Hunter's Hideaway. She'd been kind to him back then. Even kinder now. At the moment, though, her challenging gaze rested on the young woman next to him.

He turned to stare at the blonde now offering what looked to be a forced smile.

This was Rio? *Princess* Rio? The spoiled, freckle-faced ripsnorter who'd shadowed him while he did his chores, got underfoot and dared him to try to do something about it? He'd landed in trouble more times than he cared to remember for taking desperate measures to keep her out of his hair.

She thrust out her hand. "Hey, Cash. Long time no see."

Still stunned, he briefly took her surprisingly firm grip in his. "Guess it has been."

He'd been thirteen the last time he'd laid eyes on her. She'd have been—what? seven?—when his dad had been booted from Hunter's Hideaway in disgrace.

"Cash accepted an offer to fill in for J.C. this summer," Jo informed her evenly, and from the tone of her voice he got the sneaking suspicion she expected her granddaughter might object to that decision. But why? Surely Rio didn't hold it against him that her cousin had once talked him into locking her up. Not that it had required much persuasion.

"Then," Jo continued, "if all goes well—which I expect it will—he'll move into the managerial role when you leave."

Wait, wait, wait.

Little Rio Hunter—okay, not so little now—was the manager of the Hideaway's horse operation?

During the interview, Jo had talked in general regarding a current manager's imminent departure—J.C., he'd assumed—and expectations for the position. Then she'd touched on the summer hires. And she'd mentioned that a potential events booking agency would soon be inspecting the family-run business, including the horse-related part of the outfit. Rio's name hadn't come up. He hadn't seen her when he'd toured the facilities.

But did that mean he'd be...?

"Looks like you'll be reporting to me, Mr. Herrera." Deep blue eyes that a man could get lost in gazed up at him with a hint of amusement.

Reporting to the *Princess*? *When pigs fly.* He glanced at Jo, seeking confirmation that there was a misunderstanding.

"Temporarily," the older woman assured. "Rio departs in August."

Two and a half months. Not exactly what he had in mind when he'd decided to leave wrangling at a dude ranch in hopes of bettering his financial situation, but he could live with that, seeing as how he didn't have much choice. Not if he wanted to give his son a home and gain legal custody.

Speaking of which…he glanced out the door Rio was still holding open. No sign or sound of Joey. He'd better get moving.

"If you don't mind, I need to track down my boy."

"Then let's plan to meet at the main barn at 5:00 a.m. tomorrow." Rio's chin lifted slightly. "You'll have plenty to learn in a short time about how we do things here."

A muscle in his gut constricted. He couldn't leave Joey by himself at that hour. When he'd applied for the job last month and then interviewed earlier this week, kid care hadn't been part of the equation.

Jo shook her head. "Not tomorrow, Rio. Cash needs time to make childcare arrangements and get his son settled."

"He can't take care of that today? Saturday will be busy, and we can't have a kid running loose around here." Rio crossed her arms, clearly irritated and wanting to get the show on the road, even though she apparently hadn't even known he'd been hired until a few minutes ago. "Not only does Cash have a job to do, but there are too many dangers a boy can get into if left on his own."

She sounded as if she didn't think he was aware of that possibility. With Joey evading him right under her nose, was his amateur parenting status obvious?

"He won't be running loose," Jo assured her granddaughter. "As I've mentioned to Cash, Luke's Anna and a few of her high school friends want to pick up extra money this summer by babysitting the children of Hideaway guests. What's one more?"

Childcare. That was another expense on top of child support until he could track down his ex-wife—an endeavor he didn't look forward to—and get things legally ironed out. Sure, her new husband—the second since she'd divorced Cash—didn't want a boy around who didn't belong to him. But typical of Lorilee, in the blink of an eye she could change her mind about the new marriage *and* the hasty disposal of their son. He didn't trust her not to rethink her decision and call the law down on him for child abduction or something equally crazy.

Like her accusations of assault when he'd told her he planned to seek legal custody of Joey.

All he had now to stake a claim to his boy was a sack of personal documents with a scribbled note from Lorilee delivered by his former mother-in-law. The woman had dumped her grandson off at his place two days ago as he was readying to leave for Hunter Ridge.

"A babysitter on the premises would be great," he acknowledged. But except for his pickup, which he had to hang on to, he didn't have anything to sell for ready cash. Having lost his job at a horse training facility while jailed three-and-a-half years ago, he'd sold his two horses to help cover child support during those six months. He'd dig deep and come up with the money, though. Somehow.

But first, he had to find his boy. Who knew where the kid had gotten off to while his dad stood lollygagging with a pretty woman? "Maybe we can get together tomorrow, Rio. You know, once Joey's settled in."

She nodded, but clearly wasn't on board with his apparently unexpected arrival—which was confirmed when she gave her grandmother a pointed look.

"Do you have a minute when I could speak with you, Grandma? In *private*?"

"Come by my office after lunch."

He could guess the topic of that conversation, but if the delay didn't suit her, Rio hid it well.

Jo turned to him with a warm smile. "Welcome back to Hunter's Hideaway, Cash. We're looking forward to working with you for a good long time."

Her gaze briefly touched on her granddaughter, then she crossed the lobby and disappeared down a hallway.

When Cash turned to Rio, he caught her eyes narrowed on him in speculation—and a hint of female interest that caught him off guard. If it wasn't for the sudden flush on her cheeks when his eyes met hers, he'd think he imagined it. Princesses didn't usually look at Herreras with interest.

He shifted uncomfortably as they openly sized each other up. This situation had the makings of a complicated employer-employee relationship for more reasons than one. "I'll be in touch as soon I get the childcare arranged. But right now I need to—"

"Look, Dad! He likes me!"

To Rio's relief, their locked gazes released as they turned to the now-giggling, black-haired boy who'd earlier made a mad dash out the door. He hopped up on the low porch, a German shepherd at his side licking him every inch of the way.

"See, Dad?"

The gleam in his dark brown eyes reminded her of

the boy his father had once been. *Cashton Herrera a dad. Unbelievable.*

Cash joined them on the porch, crouching to playfully tug on the bill of the boy's baseball cap before roughing up the dog's glossy coat. The excited canine made a tongue swipe in his direction, but a laughing Cash dodged it, then stood. Rio watched the lively exchange with mixed emotions, finding it difficult to reconcile that the gentle hand on the boy and dog had once fisted in anger against an ex-wife...

Joey looked at his father with a sweetly dimpled smile, eyes bright with hope. "Can I keep him?"

"I imagine he has a home." Cash glanced at Rio for confirmation.

"He does. His name is Rags, and he belongs to my brother Luke and his family. But you'll be seeing him, Joey, if Luke's daughter Anna babysits you."

A cloud descended over the boy's expression as he eyed Cash accusingly.

"I don't want a babysitter. I want to hang out with you, Dad." He looped an arm around the dog's neck. "And Rags."

Cash's gaze flickered momentarily to Rio, then back to his son. "We'll hang out together. But I'm here to work with the horses, so we can't be together all the time."

"But—" The anxious-eyed boy glimpsed Rio watching him and self-consciously halted, giving the dog a hearty squeeze.

Sensing his distress, she offered an encouraging smile. "Do you like horses as much as your dad does, Joey?"

She'd noticed he wore tennis shoes and shorts. A

Phoenix Suns tank top. Not a miniature of Cash in that respect.

The boy shrugged, not meeting her gaze. "Dunno."

"You don't?" Rio cast a doubtful look at his father.

"There hasn't been much opportunity," Cash responded as he looked thoughtfully at his son. "But we're going to make a horseman of you yet, aren't we champ?"

Joey nodded, but without much enthusiasm, his grip further tightening on the dog so that it struggled to pull free. It was hard to imagine a child of Cash Herrera not being exposed to horses from the crib onward. Most kids liked horses, though, didn't they? If not, it might make for a long summer for the little guy.

And his dad.

At that moment she sensed Cash stiffen. Curious, she glanced in the direction his attention had focused, then she stifled a groan. Braxton and Luke were still standing by the deputy's vehicle and now looking their way.

So what did the deputy want this time? To ask her out for coffee or to the library book sale? Or was he here to pester her again to train that new horse of his? Why couldn't he get it through his head that she wasn't interested in him?

"Cash!" Luke called over, then said something to the deputy at his side before motioning Cash to join them.

Puzzled, she glanced at the man standing rigidly beside her. Eyes alert. Jaw tight. Pulse thrumming at the base of his throat. Then abruptly he stepped off the porch and halted on the other side of his son in an almost protective move.

What was…?

Deputy sheriff Braxton Turner's voice rose authoritatively. "I need a few minutes with you, Mr. Herrera."

Chapter Two

Lorilee hadn't wasted any time.

Muscles tensed, Cash stood between Joey and the two men facing him across the parking lot, his instincts at peak alert. Like the last time, would he be arrested? What would happen to Joey? Would they haul his boy off to social services or deliver him to his irresponsible mama's doorstep—wherever that might be?

Please God, this can't be happening. Not again.

And not here, not smack in the same place where his father's sorry behavior had gotten the whole family kicked off the Hunter property. Cash had taken a big risk accepting a position where people would remember his dad and judge *him* by that long-cast shadow. But this was by far the best job offer he'd gotten. Did the deputy, not much older than Cash, come from around here and recall the legacy of Hodgson Herrera?

Heat coursing up the back of his neck, aware that Rio and his son were watching curiously, he forced himself to take a calming breath as he strode across the parking lot to where the men stood.

As he cautiously neared, a grin suddenly appeared

on the red-haired deputy sheriff's face. The man thrust out his right hand.

"I'm Braxton Turner, friend of your buddy Will Lamar."

Cash's gaze flicked from one man to the other. Both the deputy and Luke Hunter were smiling, with no undercurrent of anything that might threaten him or his boy. He shook the man's hand with a firm grip that didn't acknowledge a need to show deference to the badge.

"I was chattin' with Will last night," the deputy continued, "and he mentioned you'd be in my neck of the woods. That I should come on over and introduce myself."

This was a social call?

Or was Deputy Lamar—his friend and ally since that last arrest—having second thoughts concerning him moving so far from his oversight? Was he passing the baton, so to speak, to another officer of the law?

"Will roped you into checking up on me?"

The deputy laughed. "Actually, I was bemoaning to him the bad habits of a mare I recently picked up at a bargain price. Wild Card's living up to her name, a real handful. Rio won't touch her with a ten-foot pole, but Will said you'd be the man to see."

Was that the truth? That's all this was?

The tension in his shoulders eased slightly. He scuffed a toe in the dusty gravel, anchoring his mind to the present, reining it in from alarmist excursions. The man wasn't here to arrest him for child abduction. To take Joey away.

Cash offered what he hoped was a relaxed smile. "Bargain price, was she?"

The other man chuckled. "For good reason, I soon

found out. Think you could give my new nag deportment lessons?"

Cash rubbed the back of his neck, kneading still-tight muscles. Always enjoying an equine challenge, he'd love to get his hands on the ornery horse. Success there might further enhance his growing reputation as a horse trainer, as well. But first things first. He got the distinct impression his primary mission would be proving himself to Rio Hunter. "I arrived this morning, so my time's not yet my own. You probably should talk to Rio about my availability if the horse needs attention right away."

The deputy glanced in her direction and, if Cash wasn't mistaken, there was a glimmer of interest in the lawman's eyes he didn't much care for. Not that it was his business, but an unexpected protectiveness welled up for the sassy little girl he'd once known. He didn't know her now, though. And, like Lorilee, it appeared she might have a string of love-struck males queued up awaiting her beck and call.

The man's smile widened. "I just may have a word with her, then."

Cash, too, glanced back to where Rio now crouched next to his son. Having gotten the German shepherd settled down between them, she was talking quietly to the boy as they patted the animal, effectively distracting Joey from what was going on with the deputy and his dad. His heart swelled with gratitude.

But what was she finding to talk to the boy about? With prompting, kids could be blabbermouths. He didn't need the whole world knowing that up until now he hadn't played as much of a role in his son's life as he'd have liked. Even now he was clueless as to where to start.

"So what do you think of mountain country, Cash?" Drawing his attention from the woman and the boy on the porch, the deputy folded his arms and leaned back against the door of his SUV. "Quite a contrast to the Valley of the Sun where you hail from."

Cash's law-enforcement friend obviously hadn't filled Braxton in that he wasn't entirely a stranger to this more-than-mile-high forested territory well north of Phoenix, and Cash breathed easier. Horse business. This visit from a deputy amounted to nothing more. But he'd touch base with Will as soon as he could. Let him know of the potential legal hot potato of Joey's arrival. He should have done that sooner. But he'd been reluctant to risk being advised not to relocate until the custody transfer was finalized.

"Pine country," Cash agreed, "sure beats the one hundred degrees the Valley hit yesterday."

Through the rolled-down window of the county vehicle the deputy's radio crackled to life. Braxton jerked open the door, slid in behind the wheel, then buckled his seat belt. "Duty calls, gentlemen. Good meeting you, Cash. I'll be in touch. See you around, Luke."

As the SUV pulled away, Rio's older brother again welcomed Cash to the Hideaway, then headed off in the direction of a crew-cab pickup. Still wound tight, Cash nevertheless gratefully returned to the main Hideaway building.

Talk about a close call.

It underlined the importance of getting legal custody. He couldn't live like this on a daily basis, never knowing when Lorilee might rethink things and turn on him. Nor did he want his heart knotting every time Deputy Turner's vehicle pulled in at the Hideaway. And from the man's expression when he looked in Rio's direction, he'd be back often.

Rio rose to her feet as he approached, her gaze cautious. "Everything okay?"

She would have been out of earshot of the conversation, left in the dark. How much her grandmother had shared with her regarding his past run-ins with the law, he didn't know. But probably at least some of it, which would account for the look of concern at the deputy's need to see him. And maybe, too, why she didn't seem overly thrilled with his acceptance of the job.

Despite what his record showed, though, he'd never struck a woman. And he'd never hit a man who hadn't swung at him first. But that was behind him. He was a changed man from the inside out, although it might take time for others to recognize and accept that.

"As you know, the deputy has a horse needing work. A friend of mine who knew I was signing on here pointed him my way. I told him he'd need to speak with you before I could take that on."

Rio rolled her eyes in apparent exasperation. "It's fine with me if you want to give it a shot, but you're at least the fourth person he's asked to tackle that horse, me included. The mare is beyond beautiful, but Brax won't admit he needs to divest himself of a bad investment and move on."

"What seems to be the animal's problem?"

"You name it, she specializes in it." She ticked off the offenses on the fingers of one hand. "Biting. Kicking. Balking. Bolting. Talk about headstrong."

Watching her animated expression as she related the horse's shortcomings, Cash raised a brow. "Sounds like a little girl I used to know."

Brought up short by his teasing tone, she stared at

him for a long moment. Then a hint of a smile touched her lips. "Very funny."

"You gotta admit, Princess," he said, enjoying the sudden flash of irritation in her eyes when that long ago nickname rolled off his tongue. "You were trouble with a capital T."

"Don't go princessing me, Cashton Herrera." She indignantly tossed her ponytail over her shoulder. "You're one to point fingers. Between your and my cousin's pranks, it's a wonder I wasn't permanently traumatized."

"You held your own, and you know it."

She cut him a look out of the corner of her eye. "I can still hold my own, and you'd better never forget it."

"Wouldn't dream of it." He was serious, too. Years ago he'd learned never to turn his back on her if it could be helped, and he wasn't starting now. He'd do whatever he had to do to stay on her good side in the coming days.

While accepting this job was risky, it looked to be the fresh start he needed. A significantly increased income. Responsibilities he could sink his teeth into. It had the potential to be his dream job with a future, even though it landed him back in one of the many places he'd had no intention of ever returning. To a town where he—and no doubt plenty of others—could still smell the lingering stink of his no-good father.

"I understand your concerns, but I have reason to believe Cash will be a good fit," Grandma Jo assured her for what seemed the hundredth time since Rio appeared at her office door an hour ago. "You're like I was at your age. Restless. Independent. Wanting to strike out on your own. Bringing Cash on will allow you to do that."

But Grandma's striking out on her own had involved

marrying Rio's grandfather and joining him in overseeing Hunter's Hideaway. Not exactly the same thing as Rio's desire to, as her brothers teased, "save the world."

"I don't think Cash is the best we can do."

"So you're willing to stick around indefinitely to give us more time to drum up and try out additional candidates?"

"That hardly seems fair, does it?" She'd had everything worked out months ago with her cousin J.C., only to have his abrupt departure and her own looming one send her Grandma Jo scrambling to find someone to take over the management of a critical segment of the family operation. Grandma had nixed Rio's suggestions of pulling Grady back in to oversee it. He'd moved on to other business-related responsibilities.

"Well, then, there's your answer. Cash is our man."

She wasn't leaving her granddaughter grounds on which to further an argument, but Rio had to give it one final try. "Did you know he was bringing a kid, or did he just show up with one?"

"I didn't know initially, but he did call ahead to confirm that bringing his son was okay. I assured him it was. So, sweetheart—" Grandma Jo put her arm around Rio as she walked her to the office door "—even if you were willing to delay your departure, an offer has been made and accepted. Give Cash the benefit of the doubt and focus on getting him up to speed on our operation. Not only are we preparing for that events contractor's visit, but in a week we'll see a big uptick in guests coming from the Valley and elsewhere for a cool weather retreat."

"I know the drill, Grandma. I've lived and breathed it since I was old enough to sit on a horse."

"Then take care of business here and before you

know it—" Grandma gave her a hug "—you'll be free to take care of business elsewhere."

So this *wasn't* a ploy to get her to stay after all. Could it be that the whole family was tickled pink to see her depart?

When a disheartened Rio entered the lobby, her mother was manning the front desk. At sixty-one, Elaine Hunter looked amazing in jeans and a light, mint-green sweater. Nobody who didn't know the shoulder-length sandy brown hair was a wig would ever guess she'd been battling breast cancer since early last fall.

Rio's heart swelled with love. "Hey, Mom."

"Hi, honey." Her mother's face lit up at the sight of her. "I'm sorry I missed you when you got back this morning. Then I had lunch with your dad in town."

"Grady told you I needed to see Grandma, right?"

She nodded, her gaze probing. "How did that go?"

"As expected, I guess. I was basically instructed to forget the fact that her new hire has a past we don't need in our present. Just keep my chin up and carry on."

"That's how your grandmother's dealt with life— the death of her parents when she was a teen, the loss of an infant child, your grandpa's sudden death. It's not a bad thing."

"I'm not saying it is. It's just that…" If only someone understood. Understood why Cash *wasn't* a good fit.

"It's that," her mother echoed quietly, "you don't want to look back on your departure with regrets."

Rio searched her mother's eyes. Having come face-to-face with her own mortality this past year, did Mom look back over her life with regrets? Things she wished she'd done—or hadn't done? Things she might not now have time to do?

But far more than the fear of regret was now driving her daughter. Rather, it was a secret she'd never told anyone—that when Mom was diagnosed with breast cancer last September, Rio had told God she'd make her own life count for Him in exchange for Him saving her mother. That she'd no longer ignore the earlier inner promptings to devote herself to counseling those who—like her—were victims of all-too-common dating violence.

As much as she loved her family, the horses and the Hideaway, what she was doing here now fell far short of fulfilling the vow that kept her mother safe.

"Rio!" One of her two sisters-in-law waddled—for want of a more flattering word—into the lobby, her arms filled with pillows and bedding. With a huff of breath from the exertion, she plopped them atop the front desk. "You're exactly the person I need to see."

Rio eyed her warily. "What's up?"

Shaking back waves of long blond hair, a weary-looking Delaney Marks Hunter slipped her hand protectively over a well-rounded belly. Rio's formerly widowed brother, Luke, was ridiculously proud of that upcoming addition soon to put in an appearance not even a year after he and his new bride tied the knot.

"Someone needs to take these out to the new hire's cabin. There's a double bed, but Grandma Jo's also having a single rollaway delivered for his boy." She patted the stack. "That's quite a hike for me and Junior here... so we're looking for a volunteer. Any takers?"

"Do I have a choice?"

"Very funny, but you don't fool me, Rio. I caught a glimpse of that guy this morning when he was here to see your grandma. *Whoa.*" Delaney fanned her face with her hand. "I can't imagine dropping this stuff off will be too much of a hardship."

Rio made a face. No doubt female guests at Hunter's Hideaway would more than approve of Cash. Admittedly, there had been a time when she'd have been hyperventilating in the presence of a good-looking, well-built man like him. But she'd learned her lesson. God looked not at the outside of a man but at his heart, something she was learning to do, as well.

And as far as *she* was concerned, any man who'd struck a woman had the darkest of hearts imaginable.

But there was no point in going into that with Delaney. Rio lifted the bedding off the front desk and pulled it into her arms, noticing that her sis-in-law, mindful of the cool nighttime temperatures at this higher-than-Denver elevation, included light blankets. "I'll take care of it."

Delaney's eyes twinkled. "Cabin 10. Junior and I both thank you."

Once outside, Rio chose to walk rather than drive and followed the perimeter of the parking lot, diving off into the trees to pass by the barns and corralled horses that made up her world. The familiar scent of horses and hay, as well as a horse's welcoming whinny as she strode by, tugged at her heart. She'd miss them. But God had more important plans for her life now.

Branching off from the horse facilities, she entered a pine-lined, winding trail that led to bunkhouses and cabins sheltering employees of Hunter's Hideaway. Overhead a raven squawked, and afternoon sun filtered through the pine boughs. She found her steps slowing as her mind wandered, trying to piece together what she knew of the grown-up Cash and his son.

Cash wasn't wearing a ring, for one thing. She'd checked that out immediately, much to her shame. So he was a single dad who'd once punched out his ex-wife. But how was a man with his background able to gain custody of Joey?

Lost in thought as she continued past the cabins scattered along the trail, she was brought up short as someone behind her shouted her name. She spun to look back at one of the cabins, its door now standing open, and a hatless Cash on the porch staring in her direction.

"Are you looking for us?"

"I am." Her face warmed as she backtracked, noting as she approached the number "10" prominently tagged on the porch railing that she'd obliviously strolled right by. "Has the rollaway been delivered yet?"

"It has." He stepped off the porch. "I've rearranged the furniture so Joey will have a corner to call his own."

She handed off the bedding, noticing a dusky, masculine shadow gracing Cash's determined jaw. It gave him a rugged appearance and yet, without his hat, he looked surprisingly boyish. Even vulnerable.

With effort, she shook off the beguiling impression. "Have you had a chance to talk to Anna about sitting Joey?"

"Yes, and she's interested." His forehead creased. "Unfortunately, she's tied up this weekend with church youth group activities. And although Joey's school has already dismissed for the summer, classes here don't let out until Memorial Day weekend."

Great. A full week. She plopped her hands on her hips. "So what's the plan?"

"Anna doesn't want to be passed over for the job, so she's going to talk to her stepmom. See if maybe she'll fill in until Anna's available."

Rio shook her head. "Cash, her stepmother is almost eight months pregnant and looks and feels every day of it."

"Anna didn't mention that."

"What were your plans for childcare when you applied for this position?" Surely he hadn't thought a kid that young could be left on his own.

Cash glanced back at the open cabin door, then lowered his voice. "Childcare wasn't an issue at the time I applied."

They'd received his application a few weeks ago. So had he only recently gained custody?

"Well, we're going to have to figure *something* out." Her gaze met his, and her face warmed as hope sparked in his expressive eyes. "I mean, you are."

He shifted the bedding in his arms. "I preferred the promise of assistance in that 'we.'"

White teeth flashed in contrast to his warm complexion, a smile that had probably broken more than a few female hearts. But if Cash thought he could walk in with nothing but a cowboy swagger and an engaging grin and have her eating out of his hand, he had another think coming.

"Your kid, not mine," she quipped, not caring for the way her heartbeat had ramped up a notch at that engaging smile. But the sooner she could get Cash brought up to speed the better, or she'd never get away from this place. Like it or not, it looked like this childcare problem would take a team effort after all.

Suddenly feeling the need to put some distance between them, she moved a short way down the trail, then paused. "Let me check around. See what options I can turn up."

"I'd be much obliged."

He looked genuinely relieved, but despite Grandma Jo's support, was bringing him on a good idea? Even aside from the looming events contractor's visit and a child underfoot, was he the right man for the job? Could he be trusted?

And yet…there *was* that business about not judging others so you wouldn't be judged yourself. Grandma had pointed that out more than once in their postlunch tête-à-tête.

"Cash?"

"Yeah?"

"It's not my intention to revisit the past. But I know none of what happened with your dad when you were here before was your fault."

Chapter Three

Cash tensed. Why was she bringing that up now?

If nothing else, it was a continued reminder that while people didn't blame him for his father's sins, they wouldn't be quick to forget where he'd come from. That they'd be on guard, watching for him to make a wrong move.

He stepped back up onto the porch and carefully placed the bedding on one of the rockers, then approached a wary-looking Rio, who now stood a comfortable distance from the cabin and the possibly listening ears of his son.

"No," he said as he looked down at her, again noticing a slightly crooked nose, evidence that at some point the tough little tomboy must have taken a tumble. But it lent her pretty face a bit of whimsy. *Whimsy.* Not exactly a word found in his usual vocabulary, but it fit Rio. "No, none of it was my fault."

She darted a look at the cabin and further lowered her voice. "Nevertheless… I think I should warn you that Jeb Greer still works here. His son Eliot's back for the summer, too. Jeb was, you know—"

"Yeah, I know."

Greer. The man whose wife had an affair with Cash's father. That discovery, along with a related fistfight provoked by the behavior of Cash's dad, had Jeb's wife fleeing the scandal and gotten the Herrera family thrown off the Hunter property.

While his thirteen-year-old self had cringed with every blow as that fight played out, a reluctant admiration for his wiry-built old man had nevertheless swelled as Cash had watched him expertly duck, sway and dodge. Then a one-two punch sent blood gushing from the nose of his bigger, burlier opponent. Caught up in the unfolding spectacle, Cash had laughed, fist punching the air in triumph. That was, until he caught the hate-filled look on the face of the other man's ten-year-old son.

Their gazes had met and held, and in that moment Cash's young heart knew he'd made an enemy for life. Justifiably, he was soon to learn, once he discovered the reason for the fight.

Cash shook off the recollection, determining to do his best to steer clear of both father and son. No point in his presence dredging up bad memories for them. "Thanks for the heads-up."

She nodded and he turned toward the cabin, then paused to look back at her. "How'd that turn out? For the Greer couple, I mean. Did she come back?"

"Divorced."

Not unexpected.

"Sorry to hear it." He knew well the wound Jeb lived with—despite the passage of time—when a woman he'd taken into his heart betrayed him. He'd ridden that trail himself. Wasn't inclined to risk riding it again.

Rio waited for him to continue, but that wasn't a topic he intended to pursue. Instead, he raked his hand roughly through his hair. "Look, I apologize for this kidcare obstacle. I appreciate your offer of assistance. But do you think maybe, for the time being, Joey could come along with me? That way I can get started tomorrow. Not delay things."

She gave him a doubtful look. "You want a kid to tag along who isn't sure he even likes horses?"

He hadn't figured out what was going on with that. Joey *claimed* he wasn't afraid of them.

"He may not be into horses—yet—but there's nothing stopping him from sitting on a barrel and playing with his trucks. Or mucking out stalls and filling water tanks. At eight years old I was doing that and more. You were, too."

"I don't know, Cash…"

He watched with bated breath as she nibbled the corner of her lower lip in concentration. *Princess Rio*. Who would have imagined fourteen years ago that the little snip would blossom into such a head turner? But since he'd clued her in that at the time of his application childcare hadn't been an issue, she was probably questioning how well he knew his son. Wondering if he could vouch that Joey would cooperate when accompanying him.

In all honesty, he didn't know.

It might take some doing to roll the little guy out of bed before dawn, but although she hadn't done the hiring, he sensed it would be to his long-term advantage to have Rio's seal of approval. Starting tomorrow would be a point in his favor.

"So what do you say?" he prompted. "I think we both want to make this transition work."

She slowly nodded, as if not yet convinced. "I guess

it wouldn't hurt. Maybe we can try it tomorrow, anyway."

"That's all I ask."

Her mouth curved. "Not asking much, are you?"

With a sense of elation that he'd won her over, he couldn't help but share her smile as they openly studied each other, her mind likely teeming with as many questions about their working relationship as filled his. If he guessed right, this spunky lady kept many a man—the deputy?—on his toes these days, and not because they were on guard for an ambush as he'd often been in his youth.

Looking down at her, he caught the soft, quick intake of her breath before she abruptly spun away and started down the trail back to the heart of the Hideaway.

"See you at sunrise," she called over her shoulder with a sassy toss of that ponytail, and he shook his head. This might prove to be a long—and interesting—few months. But as he headed back to the cabin—his and Joey's new home—a soul-deep gratefulness welled up within him.

Everything works for the good for those who love God and are called according to His purpose.

Three years after he'd joined God's team just prior to being released from jail, he was still trying to get his head around that biblical promise—a vow that God would bring good from the worst of situations.

Wasn't his friendship with Deputy Lamar proof of that? And the job he'd landed at the dude ranch shortly thereafter? Even working with horses as his dad dragged the family from job to job—from affair to affair—on ranches and at other horse facilities had come full circle. He'd acquired the experience to gain a foothold at Hunter's Hideaway. And now, in time for

Joey's arrival, this job came with the added bonus of
lodging that hands-down beat his bunkhouse quarters
at the dude ranch where he'd previously worked.

God was looking out for him. For them.

Joey met him inside the door, his brown eyes
anxious—an expression that regularly alternated with
a pugnacious one. It had been good to see him laugh
with the German shepherd earlier that day. But had the
boy, in his father's brief absence, thought his daddy had
left him on his own like his mother had been known to
do? Abandoned him as it might seem his grandma had
done two days ago?

"Hey, champ." He placed a hand on Joey's head,
ruffling his hair. The child wasn't much into hugs, and
Cash tried to respect that. Wasn't into saying "I love
you, too," either, no matter how many times his father
told him he was loved. But at the moment it was hard
not to pull him close to his heart. "What's up?"

The youngster's jaw jutted, dark eyes uncertain. "I'm
going to live with you forever now, Dad?"

Is that what his boy wanted? Didn't want? He hadn't
been overly talkative since his grandma dumped him
off. Hadn't spoken a word about his mother, either. Only
occasionally did a betraying flash of temper surface to
express an underlying anger and confusion he wasn't
yet ready to verbalize.

More than anything, Cash longed to tell him yes,
they'd be together forever. But he had no legal right to
his son yet. Not unless his ex-wife honored her hastily
scribbled note that Cash's former mother-in-law had
entrusted to his care. If he told Joey they'd be living together from now on, would that make him feel further
forsaken by his mother? Or if he was okay with living
with his dad, would an affirmative answer set him up

to have his hopes dashed if Lorilee or the law subsequently refused to allow it?

"That's what I'm praying for." He gave Joey's shoulder a reassuring squeeze. "That is…if that's what you want."

"Whatever."

The boy pulled away. Not exactly the response Cash was hoping for.

"You know," he ventured, doing his best to sound reassuring, "I'm here to listen anytime you want to talk."

"Talk about what?" Joey looked at him with a deliberately blank expression. The Dead Eye Look, Hodgson Herrera called it. A stare that, had Cash pulled it on his own father, would have gotten him knocked halfway across the room.

But Cash drew a slow breath, determined not to let the child light a fuse under his own sometimes volatile emotions. Joey had every right to be angry. To not trust him. "We can talk about anything you want to, whenever you want to."

"Nothing to talk about."

One. Two. Three. Counting to ten—even twenty— had become a lifesaver these past three years, and Cash felt the tension slowly ebbing. "Suit yourself. But there *are* a few things I need to talk to *you* about. Guy stuff."

Joey's eyes cautiously brightened. "Guy stuff?"

"That's right." Cash chucked him lightly on the arm. "You said you wanted to hang out with me. Well, we're going to get a chance to do that. But I'm going to need your help…"

"What are you up to, Luke?" In the near-dawn of Saturday morning, from one of the box stalls where she'd been checking in on a pregnant mare—her favorite horse, Gypsy—Rio watched curiously as her brother pulled his saddle out of the tack room. Surely he wasn't headed for a ride at this hour?

"I'm setting this out for Cash to take a look at." He placed the saddle on a bale of straw, tilting it forward to rest on its saddle horn. "This strap here is getting worn. When I ran into Cash after supper last night and he mentioned he's done leatherwork in the past, I asked him to take a look at it. See if it can be repaired."

"I'd be happy to look at it for you." She was more than capable of evaluating saddlery. Making repairs, too.

"No need. Keep on doing whatever it is you're doing there, but point Cash in this direction when he gets in."

With an exasperated sigh, she glanced at her watch as Luke departed. Ten more minutes and Cash would be late. Having lain awake in the night thinking of the too-handsome new hire and everything needing to be done before the events contractor's visit, she was now grouchy and having misgivings concerning allowing Joey to join them.

Not only did the family have planning ahead for the contractor's visit, but she and Cash also had their regular work to do. While summer hires could muck out stalls and help with the feeding and grooming of thirty horses, she enjoyed the hands-on involvement with the animals and time with the guests and wanted to evaluate Cash in those respects. Working with the horses and matching rider experience levels was especially important.

Today she'd team up with Cash as trail ride wranglers, then when they got back they'd cool down the animals, grab a bite to eat and be back to prepare for an afternoon ride. There would be no opportunity to keep track of a child, to keep him safe and out of mischief.

Lost in thought, she startled when Cash hailed her from one of the barn's wide-open double doorways.

"Here we are, with minutes to spare."

As she exited the box stall and secured the door behind her, she looked at her watch again, almost disappointed that Cash was two minutes early so she didn't have grounds to take out her crankiness on him. She couldn't help but smile as he approached, though, one hand steering a foot-dragging Joey in front of him and the other grasping a reusable shopping bag lumpy with what she guessed to be toys.

Again she noticed the boy's unsuitable attire, topped by a windbreaker on this coolish morning. Nor did she miss the way he anxiously took in the presence of the stabled horses. "You need work clothes, Joey. Jeans. Boots."

The little guy shrugged as he glumly looked up at his dad. Not a happy camper this morning.

Cash studied him. "Yeah. His wardrobe's definitely suited to a suburban desert climate. Maybe we can find a secondhand store someplace. There's no point in investing much money in something he'll outgrow overnight."

Yesterday she'd glimpsed Cash's pickup parked behind his cabin. While the aging vehicle was well cared for, she suspected he didn't have much to invest in anything right now.

"Well, let's get started." Snagging a clipboard from a recessed area in the wall, she flipped through the pages. "Looks like we don't have a full roster for this morning's ninety-minute ride. Only seven. Mostly newbies. One couple claims to be experienced riders, but while we don't want to assign them a beginner's mount that might bore them to tears, we don't want them to over-reach, either."

Cash led a sober-eyed Joey to a stack of straw bales and motioned for him to sit down. Handed him his bag. "It's been my experience people tend to overestimate their equestrian skills. You know, as if riding merry-go-round ponies at the county fair qualifies as an ex-perienced rider."

She laughed at his spot-on insight, remembering that, according to his application, he'd worked at a popular dude ranch the past several years. *After he got out of jail.* And before that, at other equine-related facilities where he'd trained horses. "You noticed that, too?"

He grinned. "All too common."

As they walked through the barn, keeping Joey in sight, he listened attentively to her reasoning behind her chosen rider and mount assignments. Through the stall bars he gave each horse a pat on the neck or a scratch under the chin, entirely comfortable in his sur-roundings.

So why wasn't she?

He didn't talk much, for one thing. Nodded occa-sionally. Asked a question here and there. And left her uncharacteristically prattling on to fill in the silence. It didn't help either that she was all too aware of him as he strolled along beside her, her senses on high alert. To her annoyance, the faint, clean scent of his soap and the occasional good-natured chuckle that rumbled from the depths of his chest sent her heart galloping.

Disgusted with her involuntary reaction—a betrayal of women everywhere who'd been lured in by charm-ing men with a penchant for punching—she hugged the clipboard to her chest. The crew would be arriving shortly to feed and groom the animals. Maybe that everyday routine would settle this unfamiliar edginess. "Any other questions?"

"I'm interested," Cash ventured with an earnest look, "in learning more details of what your grandmother shared regarding an events contractor coming to check things out. How do you anticipate that will affect what goes on in this particular aspect of the Hideaway?"

"We learned of the company's interest in including us as a possible venue for small-event gatherings maybe two weeks ago." Ideas for the visit were being bandied about. Nothing solidified. "I'm sure Luke will go over the financial reports with you as they relate to our seasonal trail riding offerings, hayrides and sleigh rides, but as Grandma may have mentioned, we're still recovering from that nationwide economic downturn several years ago. With the help of an influx of artisan newcomers, Hunter Ridge is getting there, but hasn't quite bounced back yet."

He nodded. "She touched on that."

"My brother Grady's bringing in wildlife photographers for workshops. But this is an opportunity for a considerable number of other small-group bookings if we can get a thumbs-up through this contractor. They claim that more and more of their big city clients are looking for unique, intimate venues for gatherings."

"Gatherings such as…?"

"Corporate retreats. Club getaways. Family celebrations—you know, milestone anniversaries, birthdays, graduations. Reunions. That kind of thing. The forest and wildlife we have in abundance here, along with our cabins, cookouts and trail rides would be a big part of the draw."

He folded his muscled arms—not that she was noticing.

"I seem to recall there was some of that here when I was a kid."

"Oh, there was, but this would be a more focused endeavor. Targeting that type of clientele to a greater extent for a more reliable source of income than sporadic group bookings provide."

He tipped his head thoughtfully. "Guests at the last place I worked had higher standards than dudes used to. Everyone likes to brag that they've been roughing it, but there's not a whole lot of roughing it in reality these days."

She laughed. "Glamping, you mean?"

That was the latest global trend—"glamorous" camping. Getting off the beaten path in luxury.

"No offense, Rio, but while the Hideaway provides clean, well-cared for accommodations with a homey touch, they don't exactly fit the definition of luxurious unless you're visiting from a Third World country."

Thanks for pointing that out, Mr. Herrera.

"Well, that's something we'll be discussing in-depth next week." She kept her tone deliberately light, determined not to take offense at his critical comment. "We'll be considering what upgrades or alterations might realistically be required to meet the needs of a slightly different type of guest."

"You've researched this company and asked for a profile of their clients? Have an idea of the caliber of venues the company is currently booking?"

Rio took a steadying breath. Gave him her best smile.

"I'm sure Grady or Luke have either done that or will be doing it soon." Neither had mentioned it, though. She'd been gone a week, however, and would no doubt be brought up-to-date at Monday night's weekly business meeting—of which Cash would now be a part. "But we have time on our side. The company's been candid with us that they're evaluating numerous potential sites in the West and Southwest this summer. We're one of many. They ballparked the Hideaway visit for late July. Maybe not until August."

"But don't you think—"

"Dad!"

Relieved at the interruption, she turned to where a wide-eyed Joey was still sitting on the bale of straw, now surrounded by three attentive barn cats.

"I think they want to eat me, Dad."

Did the giggle from the too-solemn boy warm his father's heart as much as it did hers?

She handed the clipboard to Cash, then trotted the length of the wide passage between the stalls. When she reached Joey, she swiftly scooped up a yellow tabby. "These fur balls don't want to eat you. They're waiting for you to give them a treat."

Extending her arm behind him to lift the lid on a small plastic box attached to the wall, she pulled out a handful of kitty treats. She gave one to Joey, who tentatively held it out to the cat in her arms. It made short work of the treat, crunching happily away. The other two jumped atop the bale with the boy.

He smiled again. "They all want some."

As the cat in her arms leaped to the floor, she sensed Cash coming up behind her and held out a treat to him. But when he shook his head, she handed the remaining goodies to Joey.

"Look, Rio," Cash said, his voice low as he pulled her aside. "I'm sorry if I came across as disparaging of the Hideaway. That wasn't my intention. It's just that

I've spent the past several years catching a glimpse of the lifestyles of the rich and not-so-famous, and it's been an eye-opener."

"I imagine so." Obviously he didn't think the Hideaway could meet those lofty expectations.

"I do have ideas, though," he continued with a nod to her clipboard still in his hands, "that may be in keeping with the integrity and history of the place."

Cash hadn't been on the premises twenty-four hours and he already had ideas?

Annoyed at his presumptuousness, she tried to ease her clipboard from his fingers. They had business to attend to.

But he didn't relinquish it.

She gave it a tug. He held fast.

Looking into his amused eyes—he'd no doubt noticed the spark of irritation in hers—she fought back the urge to jerk it out of his hands. "May I have my clipboard, *please*?"

"You may." He leaned in slightly. "But only if you forgive me for sharing my opinions. I get the feeling that, in spite of the future role I'll be playing here, you think I'm stepping out of bounds—Princess."

Heartbeat sprinting, to her irritation she couldn't draw her gaze from his. *Out of bounds.* That's definitely where he'd stepped. "I—"

"So it's not a vicious rumor," a man's voice boomed from the open doorway.

Cash immediately relinquished the clipboard and stepped away from her as the man approached. Now as big and burly as his father, Eliot Greer was dressed in work clothes and boots, his unruly blond hair shower-damp. He was a handsome man several years younger than Cash, who was at the moment looking at Eliot blankly, as though trying to place him.

But why was her face warming as if the new arrival had caught her in a compromising situation with their new hire?

"You remember Eliot Greer," she said somewhat breathlessly, "don't you, Cash?"

"Oh, yeah." Eliot chuckled, but didn't sound amused. "He remembers me."

Chapter Four

Now that a name had been put to the big bruiser of a guy, Cash could see the resemblance between the grown-up version of Eliot and his father, Jeb. Although time had passed, those pale blue eyes that had once stared holes in Cash didn't cut him any slack now as they flicked between Rio and him.

He'd have to be stupid not to recognize the disapproval in the gaze—and its softening when resting on Rio. Cash had barely set foot on the property, and already another of Rio's admirers had surfaced.

Eliot thrust out his hand. "Wish I could say it's good to see you again, Herrera."

"Been fourteen years." Cash briefly clasped the offered hand. He had no intention of reviving youthful conflicts.

Eliot's eyes narrowed. "I have to admit I'm surprised you're back in Hunter Ridge considering this is where—"

"Let's not go there." A familiar splinter of anger wedged itself under Cash's fairly thick skin—something he'd been on guard against in recent years, too well aware of where it could rapidly lead. Conscious of his son seated nearby, Cash's words came quietly. "We were boys, and our parents' poor choices had nothing to do with us."

The man snorted. "Maybe not for you, but—"

"Eliot." Her eyes issuing a warning, Rio nodded toward Joey, who, although earlier occupied with the barn cats, was now taking in the conversation with interest. "This is Cash's *son*. Joey."

The other man studied Cash's boy for a long, expressionless moment, then walked over to shake his hand. "Good to meet you, Joe Herrera. I imagine we'll be seeing a lot of each other this summer."

The boy nodded uncertainly, his questioning eyes darting to his dad. Then Eliot moved back to Cash.

"So you have yourself a kid now. That come with a wedding ring?"

Cash's jaw tightened at the insinuation that there wouldn't have been one. "It did. Divorced now."

"Figures." He gave a dismissive shrug, then turned to Rio. "I have those three wagons cleaned out and repainted. Axles oiled. So you can come around to give them your stamp of approval when you're finished with this morning's ride. See if there's anything else that needs attending to before that church group comes in for hayrides over Memorial Day weekend."

"We have a packed schedule today." She flipped through the pages on the clipboard. "I trust your work, though."

The man's chest puffed out at her words of praise. "I want to make sure things are up to the Hideaway's standards. Assuming, of course, that those high standards hold since I was here last summer."

He cut a dubious look in Cash's direction, and Rio frowned.

"Of course our standards hold. And I'll do my best to check out the wagons today."

"Much obliged." He smiled in acknowledgment, his gaze lingering on Rio. Then he gave Cash a brisk nod and strode out of the barn.

"Sorry, Cash." Rio made a face that reminded him of when she was a kid. "Eliot seems a bit touchy today."

Because Cash had been standing too close to Rio when the other man had walked in? "He never liked me much when we were kids. Can't say I blame him."

"He needs to get over it."

Pushing thoughts of Eliot momentarily aside, Cash looked to where Joey was again playing with one of the cats. If he hadn't been mistaken, his son had been uneasy that morning about spending the day around the corrals and barns. But in an effort to please his dad, he'd gone along with what they'd discussed the day before— the importance of the role he'd play in enabling Cash to get started on the new job. At least the furry felines seemed to have kept him distracted. Of course, horses had yet to be removed from the confines of their stalls. But so far, so good.

Rio tapped the clipboard with a knuckle. "Looks like we're set to go. And no rush, but later today Luke has a saddle he'd like you to—"

"How long, again, is Eliot here for?"

At his too-abrupt comment, she gave him a questioning look. "He's in college. Comes back here to work every summer. Is that a problem?"

"Just wondered." Fortunately, as the future horse operation manager, he wouldn't have to deal with the other man year-round. But would there be an expectation that Eliot be hired full-time postgraduation? "What's he do besides maintain wagons?"

"Odds and ends. He does building and fence maintenance. Is active in trail rides and hayrides. Whatever needs to be done."

"What's his major?"

She frowned, tiring of his questions as she'd earlier tired of his opinions? "Sports medicine. He's working on his master's. Why?"

Cash had taken a few night classes after high school himself, but hadn't gotten anything close to a degree. Eliot was one up on him in that respect. But, thankfully, the career path Eliot had chosen didn't sound like something he'd be putting into practice around the Hideaway in the future.

Cash shrugged. "I hope that works out for him."

And kept him far from Hunter's Hideaway. Eliot appeared to have a chip on his shoulder, and Cash didn't want to be forced to be the one to knock it off. But the guy could rest easy. Cash wasn't looking for trouble, and he wasn't campaigning to be president of Rio Hunter's fan club. Once upon a time, crazy in love, he'd played that thankless role with Lorilee longer than he should have—right up until she'd walked out of his life with another besotted fool, toddler Joey in her arms.

"Cash? Did you hear me?" Rio bumped his arm with her clipboard, drawing him back to the present. "Our summer hires will be here any minute to start working with the horses. You might want to find a place for Joey that's more out of the way."

"Yeah, sure." She was right. Sitting in the open might not be the best spot for him once activity picked up. Cash hadn't figured out what he'd do with Joey when accompanying Rio on this morning's ride, either.

When he'd suggested to Joey that he could double-up on Cash's horse, it hadn't gone over well. So he'd backed off that idea. Of course, he could always force the issue if that's what it came down to. Throw him up in the saddle and be done with it. That's what his own father, not pandering to any sign of weakness, would have done. But he didn't want to make the boy more fearful or risk humiliating him.

He walked over to Joey and placed a gentle hand on the boy's shoulder. "Let's find you a better place to hang out while I work."

"Can I bring the kitty?"

"Sure." But barn cats usually had a mind of their own.

When he had his son safely situated in an old-time surrey where he could watch the activity in the biggest corral, Cash joined Rio and a group of high school and college-aged summer hires. All were Hunter Ridge natives who were as horse crazy as he'd been at their age. A great bunch he'd enjoy working with.

But in short order, he again butted heads with Rio.

It was going to be a long day.

It wasn't Rio's imagination. Cash Herrera had an opinion on literally *every*thing that had to do with *any*thing.

After the last ride of the day, with satisfied guests sent home or back to their quarters to await dinner and with horses unsaddled, groomed, fed and turned loose in what passed for pasture at this high elevation, she was more than ready to call it a day. And put some distance between herself and the opinionated cowboy, as well.

But she had to stick around the barns until Cash returned from retrieving his son from her folks' place. They needed to have a talk concerning that turn of events. Her mom, having seen Joey racing his toy cars along the leather seat of the surrey before the first ride of the day, had taken him under her wing—despite Rio's protests. Baking cookies. A walk with Rags. Coloring pictures. Kids always took to Mom, and while she appreciated her mother's consideration for the little boy, Cash couldn't go fobbing his kid off on other people. Especially not on her mother, who still needed regular rest.

"He probably has an opinion about that, too," she said to one of the cats that was carefully cleaning a front paw a few feet away from her. With a sigh, she continued filling the water tank in the main corral.

Cash's first observation of the day, of course, had to do with the inadequacy of the Hideaway's facilities to meet the expectations of the ritzy clientele of the last place he'd worked. Next had been his insistence that anyone under eighteen wear a riding helmet despite the waiver stating the requirement was for those under sixteen. And he further changed things up by deciding one of the mares would handle better with a snaffle bit rather than a curb and that one of the geldings needed to sit things out until his bad habit of crowding the horse in front of him was corrected.

All the latter things were good. He knew his stuff. But already he was taking over.

Having turned off the spigot, she slowly cranked up the hose as she listened to the chattering of summer hires coming from the main barn while they attended to their end-of-day chores. More than once, to her exasperation, she overheard the name Cash.

It wasn't her imagination, either, that the guests on the two rides that day had deferred to him more times than not. That they directed their questions and comments to him rather than to her. Granted, he looked the part of an experienced horse wrangler with those well-worn boots, the Western hat low on his brow and that slow smile loaded with charm. Unlike him, she preferred to don a riding helmet to encourage the younger crowd to willingly accept the headgear rules. So maybe she didn't look as authentic as their guests thought she should?

Obviously, too, summer hires Sue, Kaitlyn, Micki and Deena, not many years her junior, had fallen head over heels for Cash, and he wasn't helping matters with the way he teased them and listened attentively to whatever they had to say. Which, to her way of thinking, was way more than needed to be said. Even Ned, Leon and Billy seemed to be developing a hero worship of sorts, setting cowboy hats at the same rakish angle as their new idol. When she'd complained to Delaney at lunchtime, she got no sympathy. Just a grin and a *sounds like someone's jealous to me* retort that irritated her further.

She was *not* jealous. She was a woman who had a job to do and people to supervise to make sure Hideaway guests had the best experience possible. But suddenly the whole world was being forced to rotate around Cashton Herrera.

"I know you said you wanted to see me, but you look like a thundercloud fixin' to break loose."

Startled, she looked up at Cash as he pushed off from where he'd been leaning his muscled forearms on the corral fence. How long had he been standing there while she was lost in her thoughts? Thoughts about *him*.

As he unlatched the corral gate, she gave the hose crank one final jerk. "Enter at your own risk, cowboy."

He slipped through the gate and fastened it closed, then walked toward her with that confident cowboy stride of his. Broad shouldered. Narrow hipped. No wonder he had the girls swooning. She deliberately looked away. Any man she'd ever again take an interest in had to have more going for him than that. The superficial looks and charm no longer hacked it.

"So what's up, Prin—"

"Where's Joey?"

He halted a few feet away, a smile surfacing in spite of her clipped words.

"He's playing with Chloe and Tessa. And yes," he added before she could voice the question, "they're supervised."

Chloe was Luke's younger of two daughters by his first wife, and Tessa was the child of the former Sunshine Carston, town council member, artists' cooperative manager and Grady's bride as of last Valentine's Day.

She placed her hands on her hips. "It's not going to work, Cash."

"What isn't?"

"Not having a regular caregiver in charge of Joey until after school is out. Besides, Anna usually has a full plate of summer activities—horse shows, church youth group outings, chores around the Hideaway."

"We'll work around them."

"How? My mom can't be taking on your kid to raise. No way. She's—" Maybe she shouldn't go there. Mom's health was family business and didn't concern an outsider.

"She's what?"

"She has more important responsibilities than playing babysitter."

Cash frowned. "I didn't ask her to help. You were there. She offered. Joey would have been fine right where he was."

"You think so?" She gave him a disbelieving look.

"Take it from me, that kid isn't going to be satisfied with sitting by himself for the next week, no matter how much you'd like to believe it. It's a matter of time before he gets bored and restless, and the next thing you know—"

"We made a deal."

"A deal."

"Right. I explained how I need to make a go of this job and that I need his help. That he has to stay out of trouble. He was good with it."

This man was clueless. "He's eight years old."

"And smart as a whip."

"I'm not disputing that. But a deal? I can see what you're getting out of it, but what's in it for him?"

"Well…" Cash looked momentarily perplexed, then his voice firmed. "Whatever time I have free on Sundays is his. Whatever he wants to do. Within reason, of course."

"So ten to twelve hours a day, six days a week he kicks his heels and twiddles his thumbs all by his lonesome while you go about your business."

"That's the way it has to be. For now, anyway."

"It's not going to work, and you'd know it if you'd stop to think about it."

"Then what do you suggest?"

What *did* she suggest? Besides Cash heading on down the road and out of her life? But then where would that leave her? The fall semester started in Flagstaff mid-August. The Hideaway's horse operation season wouldn't end until the middle of October when they'd ship most of the animals to lower elevation pasture. It cost too much to feed grain and hay to over thirty horses all winter. She sure didn't want to get stuck staying here until they could find a suitable replacement for Cash.

"It's a week, Rio. Then Luke's daughter can take over. Your grandma said that Anna's girlfriends were interested in picking up babysitting money, too. So once school's out, they can fill in for her as needed."

"And what if they have other plans at the same time?"

"We deal with it then. Didn't your mama tell you never to borrow trouble?"

He winked, and her betraying heart fluttered.

"I'm not *borrowing* trouble, Cash. I've found it works best to carefully evaluate situations—worst-case scenarios—and safeguard against the unexpected. I don't like being blindsided."

Blindsided. Like when boyfriend Seth Durren's steel-hard fist had crashed into her face, cutting her lip and breaking her nose. But here she stood, arguing with one of *those* kinds of men who made the world less safe for women, over something that anyone with common sense would know couldn't work.

"It wouldn't be you getting blindsided," he said, carefully studying her as if sensing a powder keg of emotions under the surface. "It would be my problem to deal with. Mine to handle."

She drew a breath. He was right. Joey had nothing to do with her. Not really. Not as long as the boy was kept out of harm's way and his presence didn't interfere with Cash's ability to do his job.

The cowboy offered a tentative smile. "So are we good?"

"I guess we have to be."

"Well, then." He gave her a brisk nod, his dark eyes reassuring. "We have a job to do. Let's get on with it."

Yes, that's what they needed to do. The summer season was here. The contracting company's visit but a few months away.

And she still had a vow to keep to God.

Chapter Five

Something poked him in the back.

Cash grunted but didn't open his eyes. Instead, he lifted himself slightly, pulled the covers over his head and did a face plant into his pillow.

Again, something poked him.

A finger. A little one. Joey.

"Dad. *Wake up.*"

Alarmed as the desperate tone of his son's voice registered in his foggy brain, he tossed off the covers and sat up, blinking at the light streaming through the windows. "What is it? What's wrong?"

"We're gonna miss church."

Church. Right. Today was Sunday.

He glanced at the clock on the stand next to his bed. Oh, man. He'd stayed up too late last night cruising the internet for information on the company that planned a visit to the Hunter property, spending time brainstorming ideas on how their expectations might be met and—*go ahead and admit it, you stupid cowboy*—contemplating for too long the complexities of Rio Hunter.

And now he'd overslept. They didn't offer trail rides on Sundays anymore, he'd been told. And fortunately

Rio was taking the morning shift this weekend to oversee equine care. They'd trade off, and it would be his turn next Sunday.

"Aren't we going, Dad? You said—"

"Yeah, yeah, we're going." He'd promised Joey last night when he'd asked his son what he wanted to do today. It seemed a neighbor of the boy's grandma had occasionally taken him to church—to Sunday school anyway—so that's where he wanted to go. For the first time in his life, Cash had a free rein to impact his son for eternity, and he wasn't going to drop the ball.

He eased his shorts-clad legs over the edge of the bed, noting the chill in the room as his bare feet hit the wooden floor. Summer in mountain country.

The Hunter family, as he'd recalled from his youth, went to a house of worship off the main road through town, Christ's Church. His mom had taken him there a few times when he was ten, until his father had said "no more." No son of his would be turned into a Bible-thumping sissy. Today the man didn't want to hear a single word regarding the 180-degree turn his son's life had taken a few years ago, refusing visits from Cash at the prison where he was now incarcerated.

Scrambling to get ready, Cash got them to church on time—barely—Joey having fortunately gotten himself dressed and fixed his own cereal. Once inside the church, a nice woman by the name of Marisela Palmer directed them to the kids' classes. Then Cash headed in the direction of the nearest exit, intent on finding himself a cooked breakfast and lingering over a cup of hot coffee until it was time to collect Joey for the worship service.

"Good morning. Didn't expect to see you here."

Turning at the sound of the familiar voice, he halted short of the door.

Rio. And she was looking prettier than any woman had a right to in a midcalf-length, tiered turquoise sundress and dainty silver-strapped sandals, her layered blond hair free of a ponytail tie.

She didn't appear the least surprised that he was bolting for the door, but then she didn't know that while he wasn't comfortable searching out an adult class yet, he'd seldom missed a worship service since landing in jail that last time. He'd been faithful in attendance, too, at the weekly men's group his deputy friend had invited him to once he'd been released.

Rio could think whatever she wanted about his spiritual condition. He'd leave it to God to enlighten her regarding his journey to Jesus if He thought she needed to know.

"I dropped Joey off for Sunday school. I'll be back for worship."

"You *could* stay for Sunday school, too, you know. We do have adult classes. Bert Palmer is doing a study on the topic of prayer, and Pastor Garrett McCrae is continuing a series on the book of John."

The pastor's name sounded familiar, but the face surfacing in his memory was that of a somewhat wild, long-haired, risk-taking teen a few years older than him. Surely not. "McCrae. You don't mean—"

She laughed. "Yes, my cousin. So you remember Garrett."

"He's a *preacher* now?"

"He's been ministering here a year and a half, and newly married by a few weeks."

McCrae, an official man of God. Would wonders never cease? Of course, there were people he'd known through the years who'd probably do a similar double take if they heard of his own turnaround. How his temper and fists had been retired from active duty.

"You're going to stay, aren't you?" she challenged, no doubt to see him squirm as he tried to talk his way out of remaining in the house of worship. Well, he wasn't squirming on that count. Hadn't in quite a few years.

"Sure," he said, noticing with satisfaction the surprise in her eyes. "That is, if you don't think folks will mind listening to my stomach gnaw my backbone. Which class are *you* taking? Prayer, right?"

"What makes you think that?"

"Everyone wants to figure out how to get more from God, don't they?"

"Prayer isn't strictly asking for things."

"No, but you'd agree, wouldn't you, that's what often lures people to that subject?"

She gave him a curious look. "Actually, I've been attending Garrett's class."

"Then I'll join you."

And that's how he ended up sitting next to the prettiest—and most fidgety—female in a packed room of all ages and, coincidentally, picking up almost exactly where the last lesson in his men's group had left off in the same book of the Bible. Or maybe not so coincidentally. If there was anything he'd learned the past three-and-a-half years, coincidences that seemed, well, *too* coincidental, probably weren't.

But he wasn't going to start believing that running into the attractive blonde that morning might mean God had a mind to move him in the direction of Princess Rio. He was in no hurry to find himself thrown into another relationship destined for failure. Especially a relationship that involved a woman who gathered as many male admirers as Rio had following in her wake after the class. Deputy Turner, hovering in the background, looked slightly bewildered as to how to make his move in the milling herd.

Once he'd retrieved Joey, Cash found a place to sit midway back and to the side in the church's auditorium where as a newcomer he wouldn't feel so conspicuous. But at the service's conclusion, there was no slipping out, for Jo Hunter had spied them and wouldn't hear of Joey and him not joining the family for lunch.

Rio didn't look all that thrilled when her grandma announced his acceptance of the invitation, but considering fried chicken and mashed potatoes beat his own specialty—boxed macaroni and canned tuna— he was all for it.

Maybe, too, he'd have a chance to share his ideas for the future of the Hunter's Hideaway with a crowd more receptive than Rio.

It had been bad enough to have Cash actually take up her challenge to join one of the adult classes—she knew he did it to unsettle her—but now here she was sitting next to him in Grandma's dining room surrounded by family. Surely Grandma didn't intend for Cash to join them *every* week. This must merely be an opportunity before tomorrow's family business meeting for him to get to know everyone on a less formal basis.

"So what do you think of our choice of pastors, Cash?" From the head of the table, her father, Dave Hunter, smiled in his direction, the corners of his eyes crinkling.

Cash passed a bowl of green beans to Rio. "Amazing grace, is all I can say."

Everyone laughed, including Aunt Suzy and Uncle

Mac, Garrett's parents—and Garrett would be laughing the hardest had he and his new bride been present. But that's how it had been from the moment Cash walked in the door. Fitting right in. Charming the ladies. Drawing respect from the men—he'd done a top-notch job on that saddle repair, according to Luke. He had everyone eating out of his hand just as if he didn't have a past that would appall any decent person.

That appalled *her*.

"Personally," Uncle Doug chimed in with a knowing nod, "I'm waiting for the other shoe to drop."

"Ever the optimist, aren't you?" Her father shook his head, exasperated, as always, at his brother's negativity.

"Never seen a skunk change his stripe."

"Neither have I," Grandma Jo, seated at the opposite end of the table, quietly agreed, "but I have seen the darkest of stains washed clean by the blood of the Lamb."

Grady laughed. "She's got ya there, Uncle Doug."

Acutely aware of the man seated beside her, Rio sensed Cash shift restlessly in his chair. No doubt he knew that he could use a good scrub down after what he'd done to his ex-wife.

She couldn't fathom a court awarding him custody of his son with that blot on his record. Or had they? Tensing as suspicion dawned, she glanced past him to Joey, who was enthusiastically diving into a mountain of creamy mashed potatoes. The boy had never mentioned his mother in Rio's presence. Had he been forbidden to?

And if so, why?

She glanced uncertainly at Cash as she dished out green beans, then passed the bowl to Sunshine on her other side. Could it be that Joey's father was on the lam with an abducted child in his possession?

A rock-solid arm brushed hers as Cash reached for a basket of rolls, jolting her from irrational speculation. Grandma had been in contact with a deputy who knew Cash. He'd know exactly where the former county inmate was now and would be aware if he'd taken off with the boy—as would every other law-enforcement officer in the state. Brax would have cuffed him, not shook his hand on Friday.

Relax, girl.

Conversation continued comfortably around the table for the remainder of the meal. Thoughts were shared on Garrett's sermon and how good it was to see him married to Jodi Thorpe. How Luke's Chloe had a birthday coming up. Then teasing speculation erupted as to how much bigger Delaney could possibly get before "Junior" put in an appearance. Should they call him Firecracker if he arrived on Independence Day?

As the laughter died down, Uncle Doug stabbed his fork into a slice of cherry pie. "Anybody given thought to that Tallington outfit's upcoming visit? How we're going to lure them in?"

The adults around the table groaned. Everyone except Cash, who sat up straighter, his interest piqued.

Dad waved off his brother. "Come on, Doug. We're thrilled with this opportunity. The timing is a godsend. But you know we don't talk business at the Sunday dinner table."

"Maybe we should. This is a big deal. Probably one of the biggest breaks we've had since well before the economy bottomed out. This isn't something we can leave to chance."

"We don't intend to." Luke pushed aside his now-empty dessert plate and slipped his arm around the back of Delaney's chair. "You'll get more than your fill of brainstorming at tomorrow's business meeting."

Rio'd been to her fair share of those often heated family gatherings. Hunters always had plenty of opinions—and not all of them meshed well. Now the equally opinionated Cash would be thrown into the mix. Oh, joy.

"Has anybody filled you in on this yet, Cash?" Uncle Doug stared down the table at the man beside her, who was whispering something to Joey.

Cash straightened. "Pardon?"

"This visit from Tallington Associates. Has anybody brought you in the loop on it yet?"

"Actually—" his gaze flicked to Rio "—Jo and Rio have given me some background. I did research online last night, too."

"You did, did you?" Doug gave a nod of approval. "So what do you think? Do we stand a chance of reeling them in?"

Oh, no. She didn't want Cash launching into his dubious evaluation of the Hideaway, how it fell short of more sophisticated client expectations. Her brain scrambled for something to divert the direction the conversation was headed.

And yet...

Maybe if she allowed Cash to point out the Hideaway's shortcomings, let him dig himself in deep with his know-it-all views, her family would recognize that he wasn't the blessing they'd too quickly come to think he was.

Cash's gaze met hers, and she offered an encouraging nod.

"You know, Doug..." Cash gave her uncle an earnest look. "I'd like to do a bit more research. I didn't get as far on it last night as I'd like. But I hope to have solid ideas by Monday evening."

Dad laughed. "You heard the man. Topic closed for now, Doug."

Most around the table nodded, relieved that the enjoyable Sunday meal wouldn't conclude with a knock-down-drag-out clash of opinions. Oh, well, they'd get the full impact of Cash's soon enough.

Not long thereafter, the gathering broke up, with the Hideaway's restaurant serving staff arriving to clear the table. That was one of the advantages of owning a restaurant. "Catered" Sunday meals.

In the lobby, Cash lingered near the door as she approached, Joey no doubt having joined her nieces at a nearby oak tree featuring a wooden swing.

"Enjoyable meal." He held open the door for her and they stepped out on the porch. "You're fortunate to have a family like that."

"I am." Although there *were* times… "Clever evasion you managed in there, not taking the bait from Uncle Doug. Once a week, we try to put the Hideaway on the back burner and give ourselves a break for a few hours."

Cash settled his hat on his head. "When your dad chided him right off the bat, I took it as a sign that wasn't anything I wanted to get dragged into."

"Good choice." But she couldn't help but feel a bit guilty for the fleeting hope that he'd open his mouth and find himself toppled from the throne of her family's favor.

He nodded in the general direction of the stables. "Do you get much pushback from guests for not operating the trail rides on Sundays?"

She sat on a porch railing, drinking in the heady scent of sun-warmed ponderosa pine. "Occasionally.

Not often. It's something Grandma Jo decided to stop offering, at least on a regular basis, a few years back when the economy hit the skids."

"You reduced a prime opportunity to boost income right at a time when the Hideaway had been gut-punched?"

She shrugged. "Grandma felt we were letting ourselves get sucked too much into a never-ending whirlwind where one day didn't look much different from another. Becoming obsessed with the bottom line, no matter the cost to our physical, mental and spiritual health. She said if God took one day of rest out of seven, it wouldn't hurt us to take our cue from Him." She smiled. "As much as is possible, anyway, when you live and work at the same place and have guests on the property year-round."

Cash nodded as he rested a hand on the support post next to her, and their gazes connected with an unexpected jolt that sent her heart skittering. Did he feel it, too? He must have, for to her relief he immediately stepped back as if goaded by an electric cattle prod.

Surely he wasn't attracted to her, was he? While catching the eye of the good-looking cowboy fed her vanity—and while it might be amusing to daydream about coming home to a man like him and stepmothering his sweet little boy—she had no intention of allowing him to turn her heart into one more conquest among what were certainly his many. She was his *boss.* Nothing more.

"Like I mentioned inside…" Cash looked across the parking lot as if gathering his thoughts. "I did do research on the Tallington folks last night. As I suspected, they're pretty upscale. Some venues they book in Colorado, Washington and Oregon do offer horse experiences Sunday through Saturday. Trail rides. Riding lessons. So there might be pressure to do that."

Before she could respond, her nieces Tessa and Chloe came racing round the far corner of the Hideaway complex, Joey trotting almost reluctantly in their wake. Both girls squealed when they spied her.

"Aunt Rio! Aunt Rio!"

At the bottom of the low porch's steps they bounced excitedly from one foot to another.

"Will you take us riding on our ponies?" Soon-to-be first grader Tessa, her brown eyes and raven hair making her a miniature of her part-Apache mother, cut an excited look at her new cousin, Chloe. Despite a few years difference in age, they'd taken to each other immediately when Tessa and her mother joined the family.

"Please, Aunt Rio?" Chloe looked to her with hope-filled eyes.

Joey hovered silently off to the side as if trying to be invisible.

"I'd be happy to do that as long as your folks are okay with it." An hour on the trail with her nieces might be the ticket to getting her mind off the Tallington visit and her plans for the fall. And firmly off Cash, as well.

"Ask your dad if you can come, too, Joey," Chloe urged. Then the two cousins dashed back into the inn to seek permission.

"Did you want to go riding with us, Joey?" Rio tried to make it sound as if it was nothing more momentous than walking around the corner to the tree swing. As if she wasn't aware that he was uneasy around horses.

The boy stuffed his hands in his pockets, avoiding her gaze. "No, thanks."

"We have gentle ponies. One that I rode when I was your age. Her name's Misty. Like the storybook pony."

He looked at her blankly. Okay, he wasn't a fan of that beloved children's series.

She exchanged a glance with Cash, who shook his head, his expression suggesting she drop the subject.

"Can I go swing, Dad?"

"For a few minutes."

When the boy trotted off, Rio placed her hands on her hips and turned to his father.

"So what exactly are you going to do about that?"

Chapter Six

"About what?"

She shot Cash an aggravated look he probably deserved for that lame attempt at dodging her question. "About a child of Cash Herrera not being into horses. So is he actually afraid of them or just not interested?"

Good question.

"He says he isn't afraid. But I suspect it's a bit of both. Fear of the unfamiliar and having no opportunity to develop an interest." That was despite the fact that when Cash had first met her, Lorilee had been a decent competitor in barrel racing events. That's how they'd met. At a county rodeo as teenagers.

"So what—"

At that moment a laughing Luke, Delaney, Chloe and Tessa poured out of the inn onto the porch, and from out of nowhere the German shepherd, Rags, dashed into their midst. Luke reached down to pat him, pausing to raise an inquisitive brow as he glanced between Rio and Cash.

"Pardon our intrusion."

Cash wasn't sure Luke was the least bit sorry. There had been a time when not many big brothers would have cared to catch their little sisters shooting the breeze with the likes of him. While there might be a few stray sparks firing between the two of them, Rio seemed as disinclined to pursue that any further than he did. So Luke didn't have anything to worry about from Cash's corner. He might want, though, to keep a close eye on Eliot, Brax and those guys at the church.

"We were just wrapping up some business." Rio, a soft flush staining her cheeks, stood. "I was thanking Cash for not letting Uncle Doug ramrod our Sunday lunch."

Luke's forehead creased as the others and the canine moved on ahead to his pickup, the two kids assuring Rio they'd be back to ride after changing clothes. "I, for one, am not looking forward to tomorrow's meeting, considering Uncle Doug will come loaded for bear."

"Surely Dad and Grandma Jo will keep him in line."

From her tone, though, Cash didn't think she was optimistic.

Luke let out a pentup breath. "Unfortunately, it's not just him. I've heard rumblings from a few members of the extended family who also have a financial stake in this, even if they're not employed here."

"Surely not Garrett. Or J.C."

"No, but a few of the other cousins are leaning toward Uncle Doug's more extreme notions. Although we're an entity with voting rights—which many on the periphery seldom choose to exercise—Uncle Doug can be persuasive when he wants to be."

"In some ways," Rio said as she gripped the porch's support post, "I wish we'd never heard of Tallington Associates."

"Now don't go saying that. This opportunity could

be a good thing if we keep a clear head. Make wise decisions."

The horn of his pickup honked.

"Guess the troops are getting impatient." He leaned in closer to his sister. "Thanks for taking Chloe for a few hours. With Anna and Travis at the youth group thing, Delaney and I'll have the cabin to ourselves. A rarity."

She gave him a push. "Then you better get going."

"Actually—" Luke gave her a sheepish grin as he stepped off the porch "—we both were thinking along the lines of naps. Delaney's not sleeping so well these days and, consequently, me neither."

Rio gave a squeal of laughter. "Oh, wow. Real life insights into the romantically exciting world of newly-weds. You make matrimony sound so irresistible. Not."

He shook a finger at her. "Yeah, well, one of these days reality will hit when you won't be laughing so hard, and I'll be the first to remind you."

The horn honked again, and she laughed as he hurried off.

Still smiling, she watched her brother climb into his truck. Gave him a wave as he pulled away. When she turned to Cash, he got the feeling from the chagrined look in her eyes that she'd forgotten he was there. "I guess I don't have to tell you I love that guy."

"That's pretty evident. Sounds, though, as if you both have concerns involving what might transpire at the business meeting tomorrow."

"Seems the best of stuff can come, like most medications that are intended to do you good, with side effects. Like the setup of Hunter Enterprises."

"I vaguely remember tales of how that came to be. Something to do with your uncle Doug's divorce and a high-powered lawyer on his ex's side who almost cleaned him out?"

"Aunt Charlotte—who was out of the picture before I came along—tried to get her claws on more of Hunter's Hideaway property and investments than what personally belonged to her former husband. So to protect family interests, Hunter Enterprises was born."

But the woman had done considerable damage not only to the family but to the town itself. Empty, boarded-up buildings here and there along the main road through town were evidence of the fallout of that decades-old retaliation by an ex-wife. Cash should probably consider himself fortunate that he hadn't more to lose than he had. Then again, Joey had been enough.

Rio's forehead wrinkled. "So...where were we when Luke barged into our midst?"

Cash wasn't inclined to volunteer the abandoned topic, but instead stepped off the porch. "Guess I'd better round up Joey. Luke and Delaney's Sunday afternoon nap sounds mighty tempting. I'll see you tomorrow."

He started in the direction Joey had headed, but Rio hopped off the porch in pursuit.

"Oh, wait. I remember."

He kept walking, but she caught up and snagged his sleeve, drawing him to a halt.

"We were discussing Joey and his aversion to horses. What's the plan there? Are you going to attempt to get him acquainted with them or let him miss out because, I assume, his mother didn't consider it a worthwhile activity?"

Lorilee *had* thought horses worthwhile before that interest got kicked to the curb in favor of a more entertaining pastime—collecting male hearts. Although she denied it, he'd long suspected her refusal to let Joey get involved with horses was a deliberately vindictive move aimed at the boy's father.

"Horses are a big part of my life." He hooked his thumbs in his belt loops. "I'd like them to be a part of my son's life, too. But my dad pushed me into things I didn't want any part of. I don't want to risk anything like that splintering the foundations of Joey's and my relationship."

"Since Joey hasn't had any exposure to horses, I suppose that means you haven't spent much time with him up until now?"

"It's not like we didn't see each other at all." She made it sound as if he'd neglected his son. "He was in the care of his mother—spent quite a bit of time with his grandmother. It was almost an eighty-mile round-trip to see him, and I went as often as I could manage."

Man, that sounded lame. As if he hadn't tried hard enough. But he'd been working his fingers to the bone to provide child support, to set aside a nest egg for custody court costs. He'd sometimes driven those many miles only to discover Lorilee or her mother had gone off with Joey and hadn't bothered to tell him, although they knew he was coming. He'd never had much in the way of established visitation rights, and he hadn't the money or the time to pursue it when Joey was small. He didn't get so see much of his son anyway, which is why he'd jumped at this better-paying job to save up for a custody battle, if that's what it came to, even though Hunter Ridge was a farther distance away.

Rio tilted that pretty head of hers, her silken hair catching the light. "So what changed?"

He didn't want to get into this, but maybe enlightening Rio would show her why it was important that he make a success of this job and balance his time with his son. "His mother got remarried—to a man who doesn't want anything to do with an ex-husband's offspring."

He didn't mention this was her third spouse, and that she hadn't bothered to marry the handful of men she'd taken up with in between.

Rio's expression abruptly softened. "Oh, Cash, how could a mother ever...? The poor little guy."

Was Joey a poor little guy because a mother and stepfather had cast him out or because he was now stuck living with his biological father?

"He's had a rough go of it." Since the very beginning, no thanks to his inexperienced father and flighty mother.

"I have to admire you for taking him on after being cut out of the picture for so long."

"There's nothing to admire." That was an understatement. "I wouldn't have it any other way."

"I suppose, though, that's why—" Her eyes met his almost apologetically.

"Why what?"

"Why," Rio said uncertainly, not sure how the warylooking Cash might take her words, "in the short time you've been here I've sometimes sensed tension between the two of you."

"It's unfamiliar ground for both of us," he stated with a defensive edge to his voice. "But don't go feeling sorry for me. This is an opportunity I've dreamed of since his two-timing mother walked out on me when he was two. But I do concede that the timing couldn't be much worse."

Rio winced inwardly. An unfaithful wife? And bad timing for sure, right when he'd taken on a new job.

"But you can understand now, can't you," he continued, "why I'm reluctant to dump my boy off for day care in Hunter Ridge at the crack of dawn each day? Why I'd like him nearby, where I can check on him as time allows, share lunch together, start to build a real relationship?"

"You're thinking these months between now and when school starts are critical, aren't you? Laying a foundation for the rest of your lives."

"Exactly."

She'd been such an insensitive jerk, letting her suspicions about the man negatively affect a precious boy. Determination welled. "We'll make this work, Cash. We'll figure something out until Anna and her friends take over."

"When I talked to your mom before lunch, she mentioned she'd be happy to continue to help out. And in spite of Delaney's advanced stage of pending motherhood, she said she could step in, too."

Relief flooded. "So they'll be taking care of Joey?"

"Actually—" he offered a wry smile "—I thanked them, then knowing you wouldn't approve of me enlisting their aid, I turned them down."

She gave herself a head slap with the heel of her hand. "I'll talk to them. Get it straightened out."

If the perplexed tenting of his eyebrows was an indication, though, Cash didn't know what to think of her sudden turnaround.

"You don't need to do that. I can call the church. See if Pastor McCrae can recommend a sitter."

"No, no. I'll take care of things here. That way Joey can remain on Hideaway property."

"That would be mighty nice."

"Okay, then, it's settled."

But Joey's situation left her *un*settled. "That doesn't address all his issues, though, does it? To establish that father-son relationship, I suggest you start laying the groundwork by building on common interests."

He chuckled. "I'm not much into Nintendo or Legos. But I guess I could give it a try."

"I was thinking of horses. Starting there."

He gave her a look that clearly conveyed his doubt. As in *what part of the kid doesn't like horses don't you get, lady?*

"Why not, Cash? It's the perfect starting place."

"We have...trust issues to work out. He has what I suspect is buried anger toward me, and forcing him to start riding wouldn't do a whole lot for that."

"Who said anything about forcing? You woo kids, Cash. You get them thinking whatever you want them to do is *their* idea."

A corner of his mouth curved upward. "Kinda how some women manipulate their men?"

She laughed. "It sounds as if you know the inside secret."

"Been on the receiving end more times than not."

"Well, it's the same with kids. Don't nag. Don't push. Convince them that what you want them to do is exactly what *they* want to do—then stand back and let them take the lead."

She looked to him hopefully, but clearly he wasn't buying it. Perceiving the source of his doubts, she hurried on before he could deliver a flat-out no. "It's true that I don't have kids of my own, but between my brothers and two older sisters, there are now eight—soon to be nine—nieces and nephews. So I've had front-row seats and hands-on practice for effective child-rearing techniques."

"I'm not sure…"

"Come on, Cash." She folded her arms, her gaze obstinately pinning him. "I'll even help."

The following evening as Rio waited for the others to arrive for the weekly family business meeting, she kicked herself for offering to assist Cash with Joey and horses. For suggesting they both start laying the groundwork by reading horse stories to him.

But, in her defense, her heart had melted when he'd told her the boy's new stepfather—and his mother—had shoved him out the door. What kind of woman would give up her child like that? And to a man who'd struck her, no less? That kind of put a new spin on Cash's slugging the woman. Not that there was ever an excuse for such as that. But maybe his "ex" wasn't entirely the blameless party as Rio originally assumed.

When Cash had balked at her offer, she'd actually argued him down. Convinced him that introducing Joey to horses—with her assistance—would enhance his relationship with his son.

Dumb. Dumb. Dumb.

She didn't need to be spending any more time than necessary with either of them.

"Earth to Rio." Grady playfully bumped her arm as he settled into the conference table chair next to her. "Spacing out there, sis?"

She made a face as she patted the iPad on the table in front of her, filled with meeting preparation notes. "We have a ton of work ahead of us."

"And opportunity if we can make a go of it." He nodded to the spiral notebook and pen he'd placed in front of him. "I've been brainstorming myself, but I'm especially interested in hearing what Cash has to share."

She refrained from rolling her eyes.

"I wouldn't put too high of an expectation on that. We've been running the Hideaway for generations. He's only worked at an upscale dude ranch for a few years."

"Nevertheless, he might bring a fresh perspective to things. Yesterday at lunch it sounded as if he'd been doing his homework."

And coming up with more of his know-it-all observations?

Mere minutes before the meeting was to start, family members filed in to pack the conference room—but Cash managed to snag the chair directly across from her. Great. He nodded to her as he set his hat in the middle of the broad oak table, then opened his laptop. At least he couldn't criticize the Hideaway's connectivity. They'd seen to that not long ago when it became clear it was a bottom-line guest expectation.

Rio's dad, as head of Hunter Enterprises, had no more than uttered the final amen of an opening prayer when everyone started talking at once. Except her. And Cash, she noted, who appeared to be quietly taking in the chaos.

"Whoa!" Dave Hunter yelled over the din, bringing the room to a startled silence. A low key kind of guy— Grady compared him to the steady-as-a-rock father on *The Waltons* TV show reruns—he didn't often raise his voice. "Time out, folks. Take turns."

Cash met her gaze, his eyes now twinkling.

Of course, Uncle Doug jumped right in with his usual bluster. "In my opinion, what happens between now and when reps from Tallington Associates show up will make or break this enterprise for years, maybe decades, to come."

He held up a hand to silence any interruptions.

"Now's not the time to stick our heads in the sand. If what needs to be done calls for major loans, we take out major loans. If it means bringing in outside consultants, architects and contractors, that's what we'll do. If it means tearing this place to the ground and building it back up, so be it."

All that in the next two months? Besides, what was wrong with keeping things the way they were? Sure, they needed upgrades, but loyal guests had been coming here for years and what appealed to them would appeal to new guests and the events contractor, too, wouldn't it? Why rock the boat?

As if sensing her thoughts, Cash gave her a knowing look, and her face heated that he'd caught her looking at him.

Luke crossed his arms. "Tearing the place down? That's somewhat extreme, don't you think, Uncle Doug?"

The older man slammed his palm on the table. "I think this calls for extreme. Like Cash here, I've been checking out Tallington Associates' website, following links to the event sites they're promoting. Believe me, we're light-years behind them. Ain't that right, Cash?"

All eyes turned to the cowboy, who warily looked up from his laptop.

"I can't pretend to be an expert on the venues I saw featured, Mr. Hunter." His gaze again flickered to hers. "But a lot depends on the long-term vision for Hunter's Hideaway. What its mission is now and what it will be going into the future."

Spoken like a diplomat.

"But you agree the other event sites run circles around ours? Like the place you worked at—Cantor Creek." Uncle Doug smiled, sensing an ally. "Tennis courts and golf courses with pros on staff. Indoor pools. Spas. State-of-the-art conference space. Five-star accommodations. Award-winning chefs."

"What I saw featured did appear to be a step above the scope of the Hideaway's offerings."

Only a step? As much as she hated to admit it, Cash was being kind. She'd explored online last night, too, and it was eye-opening.

Uncle Doug looked around the room. "You heard the man. We're talking luxury here, folks. I mean, we don't even have TVs in the cabins, claiming that's one of the charms of this place. But is it that guests don't *want* TVs or are we fooling ourselves like we did for so long with the internet connection business?"

"Yeah, but—" Luke started, only to be cut off.

"The way things stand now, we don't have a chance of getting picked up by Tallington. I can't imagine why we were contacted in the first place unless they see potential and expect us to step up and deliver." He pushed back in his chair, satisfied that he'd made his point.

Grandma Jo, silent throughout as she waited for her second son to run out of steam, nodded to Cash. "Cantor Creek, where you most recently worked, is a prestigious guest ranch. Do you see the Hideaway having the potential to be even remotely comparable?"

Cash cleared his throat, not meeting Rio's stare. He knew how she felt about his opinions. "Honestly, ma'am? I don't think so."

Grandma tilted her head. "And that's because...?"

"First off—" he looked apologetically to Uncle Doug "—the Hideaway is hours from a major airport or metropolitan area. That's a major strike against it. Second, this isn't a working ranch like the popular Arizona venues are with herds of cattle and tens of thousands of acres of western landscape at their disposal, like something right out of an old-time movie."

"We've never pretended to be that," Rio said defensively. "We started out as a home-away-from-home for hunters in the early 1900s, then gradually expanded to horsemen and hikers and even runners looking for a high elevation in which to train."

"But gathering and moving cattle are big draws at these other places," he persisted. "Cantor Creek brings in global guests who dream of the Wild West. But despite the thrill of imagining they're genuine cowboys for a few days, believe me, roughing it isn't a part of the picture."

Uncle Doug, not to be deterred, leaned forward. "We can borrow a few cows, if that'll make them happy."

Rio almost choked.

Was he serious?

Chapter Seven

Cash again caught Rio's eye and winked, instinctively knowing she wanted no part of her uncle's over-the-top concept for the Hideaway.

Or cows.

Grady, no doubt envisioning the place transformed into something unrecognizable, complete with valet parking, monogrammed robes and rose petal turndown service, offered his two cents. "Since when is there anything wrong with a little roughing it?"

That's all it took. They were off again, everyone flinging out opinions and launching into heated conversational asides. The Hunters could really go at it, but an inner prompting advised to keep his mouth shut.

At the end of two hours, they hadn't come to a consensus on the direction the Hideaway should take. He imagined that left Rio's stomach churning, for at the conclusion of the meeting she didn't linger, but instead stepped briskly out into the starlit night and headed in the direction of the horse facilities.

"Rio?"

She halted, impatiently he suspected, waiting for him to catch up. "I have a pregnant mare to check on."

"I should check on Brax's Wild Card, too. She didn't seem real happy when she got trailered in here this afternoon."

He'd gotten the go-ahead to put her in the farthest corner box stall of the building, one with a small adjoining paddock. An empty stall and lot next to her allowed her to see and hear the other horses, but she wouldn't be able to disturb them.

Rio moved off in the direction of the main barn again, and he kept in step beside her.

"Gypsy's a barrel racer?" He remembered Rio was just getting into that as a kid.

"Yeah. I got her when I was thirteen. She's retired now, though. Like me. But we had some good years in the arena."

"I noticed the barrel racing sticker in the back window of your truck and the awards in one of the tack rooms. You don't compete now? Why's that?"

"New focus. After stepping away for a few years, I'm going back to college this fall. So I can't cram one more thing into the summer. Something had to give, and that was it."

"Which school are you going to?"

"Northern Arizona University."

NAU. At the foot of the San Francisco Peaks a few hours from there. "Major?"

"Counseling."

He hadn't expected that. "I'd have guessed animal husbandry or something along those lines."

"Sorry to disappoint you, cowboy." But her accompanying laugh fell short of softening the words delivered too sharply.

He lightly touched her arm as they entered the barn.

"The upcoming visit by this Tallington group has you rattled, doesn't it?"

She halted in the dim light. "What makes you think that?"

"Picked up on it while observing you and your family tonight. Am I right?"

"I suppose so." She let out a huff of apparent exasperation. "I don't like wasting time. Whenever we start working our way toward a compromise, Uncle Doug muddies the waters again. He won't be satisfied until we have every inch of the property razed and rebuilt from the ground up and a New York City chef installed in a high-rise rooftop gourmet restaurant."

"The likelihood of that is slim, given how snow flies here half the year."

He sensed that she caught the smile in his voice, recognized he was trying to make her smile, too. And when one at last struggled to the surface, it kicked off an unexpectedly warm thrumming in his heart.

"Grandma Jo's long known how her second son gets a wild idea and runs with it. I'm not sure she's forgiven him for impulsively marrying his first wife and how the repercussions of that divorce impacted the family. It even deprived her of a grandson when his departing ex got sole custody. Now he sees this as an opportunity to throw his weight around. Kick up dust. Try to wrest the primary decision making away from Dad."

"He can't do that, though, can he? Not without the rest of you agreeing."

"I suppose. But you were there—he's swaying opinions. Votes. We need a solid direction, Cash. We need to decide where our investment of time and money will be made. We can't go running off in different directions and expect to gain the blessing of Tallington Associates."

"I agree. But there are things that can be done independently. Why would the horse operation be impacted by a culinary wizard in the kitchen or whether or not thread count tops eight hundred?"

She cut him a resentful look—probably for stating the obvious. "I guess that *is* true."

"Sure it is. While we wait for things to get sorted out, let's control what we can. Let's see if we can get buy-in on our vision for this segment of the business. Maybe what we present will be a starting place for coming together elsewhere."

Assuming, of course, that the two of them would be more successful in reaching an agreement on their own direction than the family had been on the rest of it.

"Think about it," he coaxed. "Then we can discuss it and come up with a plan before next week's meeting."

For a long moment, she seemed engaged in an inner battle as she considered the wisdom of his suggestion. She was, after all, still the boss. But then, to his surprise, she gave a brisk nod. "Okay. We'll talk. Tomorrow night?"

He champed at the bit to put his stamp on an operation he'd be managing in the future—but even knowing grown-up Rio for only a few days, he wasn't convinced she was ready to forfeit her influence until she had to. This would give them both an opportunity for input without the turmoil evident in the larger family discussions. Or so he hoped.

"Tomorrow it is, then. Come loaded with ideas and let's get things hammered out."

They moved farther into the barn, and from the far end of the building the blowing and stomping of an unhappy horse carried clearly. He grimaced. "Good thing I've seldom been able to resist a challenge."

"You have your hands full with that one."

"I told Brax no promises, but that I'd give it a shot." She groaned. "He needs to give it up."

"I get the impression he isn't one to give up easily." He deliberately caught her eye with mischief in his own. "You know, once he sets his mind to something."

Rio glanced quickly away. It was hard to tell in the dim light, but was she blushing? Could be she wasn't entirely unaware of the good deputy's interest in her. Did she return his feelings? Playing hard to get?

As he'd told himself before, though, it wasn't his business. But nevertheless…the two didn't seem like an ideal match. Then again, what did he know about good matches? Despite a promising beginning, he and Lorilee had fallen far short and had no idea how to make up for it. Counseling? Prayer? Putting the other's needs before his or her own? No, they'd washed their hands of it and moved on—or moved on as much as you can when a child was involved.

"I'll wrap up things here with Wild Card, then swing by and pick up my boy from Delaney."

And try, too, to peel him out of the work clothes he'd surprisingly taken to when they'd stopped by a secondhand shop before supper. Joey insisted on wearing them tonight. Even asked if he could sleep in them if he took off the boots.

Rio slid open her mare's stall door, and he heard Gypsy's soft nicker of welcome as he headed toward the farthest stall.

"Cash?"

He paused halfway down the aisle. "Yeah?"

"Are you reading horse stories to Joey like I suggested?"

"As a matter of fact, I am at every opportunity, thanks to the Hideaway's library. Mixed in, of course, with Bible adventures and nonequine tales as you advised." A smile crept into his tone. "I don't know how much the stories are promoting horses in his mind, but the dog ones have him begging for a puppy."

"Don't give up. It may take time."

Her lilting laugh tempted him to backtrack closer. He resisted, but was unable to banish a smile as he absorbed the one lingering on her lips. "Thanks again for offering to help with Joey and the horse dilemma. Last night I read him an illustrated, abridged version of *Misty*, and he asked a few questions about your pony of the same name."

"That's a start."

"He's curious about Gypsy's foal, too."

"Kids love baby anything."

"Guess so." From behind him, a shrill whinny reverberated through the stillness. Brax said he'd learned Wild Card was abused a few owners back. So patience would be the name of the game. "Well, I'll see you tomorrow."

"Sounds good."

While he had no intention of challenging Eliot or Brax for Rio's attention, was she looking forward to their time together as much as he was?

Cash's shadowed figure moved away, and Rio's smile slowly melted as she joined Gypsy inside the roomy stall.

That's where it had started the last time. Shared laughter. Smiles. Warm gooey feelings. Seth Durren hadn't come with a warning label—at least not one that she'd been smart enough to read until it was too late.

Gently grooming the horse, she noted the mare's swollen belly. It wouldn't be too much longer. Boy? Girl? Maybe she'd let Joey help name the baby. Or was that allowing herself to become more intertwined in the life of Cash's son than she needed to be?

Although on the alert, she hadn't seen signs of under-the-surface leanings toward violence on Cash's part. But charm could be deceitful to the max. Looking back, though, she'd had plenty of tip-offs with Seth if she'd have paid closer attention. Had gotten her head out of the romantic clouds. Had higher self-esteem. *Remembered who she was in Christ*...a valued, much-loved child who had every right to be treated like a daughter of the King.

That realization when she was looking for a means to persuade God to spare her mother's life was what had made her determined to help other young women on campus read those subtle, too-often ignored signs. The frequent calls and texts to see where you are, who you are with. Wanting you to spend all your time with him to the exclusion of others. That was endearing at first—*he's falling crazy in love with you, right?*

But then he's telling you who you can and can't see, what you can and can't do, what you're allowed to wear. Somewhere in there comes the accusations that you're cheating on him. And the name calling, making you feel bad about yourself. The pushing, shoving, the too-tight grip.

And when you got up the courage to confront him, a denial followed that any of it was happening.

It's all in your imagination, you crazy woman. Can't you see I love you?

She shuddered, pushing away those too vivid memories.

While she didn't yet perceive those signs in Cash, the jail time he came labeled with for assaulting his ex-wife wasn't exactly veiled. So no excuses this time. As tempting as it was, as flattering as it was to think he might have an interest in her, she couldn't afford to make the same mistake again.

"Like I said, Will—" having tucked Joey into bed, Cash spoke quietly from inside the cab of his pickup parked up close to the cabin "—Lorilee's mother claims she doesn't know the new husband's last name or a new phone number. Says she forgot to ask."

"Likely story."

"Yeah, that's my take on it, too. But the first name's Samuel. She let that slip."

"A first name isn't much to go on." Cash could picture the fiftyish Will shaking a head that sported a close-cropped, salt-and-pepper haircut. In so many ways, he'd been more of a father to Cash than his blood parent had ever been. "I can check the public records online, but if neither she nor the new spouse are involved in suspected criminal activity, I can't go digging around much deeper."

Meaning, as Cash suspected, law enforcement had continued to strengthen restrictions on internal database searches for anything other than official business. Privacy laws. Prevention of misuse by governmental employees. Good stuff, but he sure could have used a break here in his search for Lorilee.

Could be, too, that they hadn't gotten married yet. Or that they'd wed out of state someplace.

"I get it. I know your hands are tied if it's not a matter of public record. But I'm over a barrel. Lorilee's mother has never been my biggest fan and, complicating matters, my ex has been known to disappear for months at a time."

"But at least she hasn't disappeared with your boy this round."

Thank You, God. "But I feel vulnerable. After what she did to me last time, I wouldn't put anything past her. The day your deputy friend showed up here about his mare, it took twenty years off my life."

"Sorry, bud. I intended to let you know to expect him, but he was so wrought up with that horse of his that he beat me to it."

Or maybe he'd heard Rio was due back in town and needed an excuse to drop by the Hideaway.

"I can put you in touch with a few people who might be able to advise you," Will continued. "County and state folks who work with child custody cases."

Cash flinched. "I don't want to wave red flags under anybody's nose. Draw unwarranted attention to my situation. What if they take a hard look at my record? Decide I'm lying through my teeth about Lorilee giving him up? Conclude I'm a possible danger to Joey?"

"You're not a danger to Joey."

"But they might think it for the best to take him away from me until they can substantiate I'm not trying to pull a fast one over on them with my claims."

"That's a risk you may have to take."

"One I *won't* take. Joey's already been through more than any kid should have to go through." He heard his friend sigh. "Look, Will, I'm putting you in a bad spot, telling you this and possibly getting you dragged into a mess if it should blow up in my face."

"It's a tricky situation. I can understand your hesitancy to involve the authorities. But you need to protect yourself—and Joey. At least retain a lawyer, Cash."

How much were lawyers' billable hours these days? Even with court-appointed representation, his last tangle with the legal system had fairly wiped out all he'd set aside in hopes of challenging his ex-wife in court. Things got better after Will took an interest and got him on at Cantor Creek, where Will's brother headed up security. But he guarded that growing nest egg diligently and hated to prematurely throw it away. Nevertheless...

"Any recommendations?" He knew he was asking a lot of his friend. Might be putting him in professional jeopardy.

"Let me check around. I'll get back with you. But in the meantime, if Lorilee turns up, absolutely do not agree to meet with her alone. Maybe not even without legal representation."

When they finished their call, Cash climbed out of his pickup truck, careful not to slam the door. He glanced toward the softly lit cabin, then up at the starry sky. As always, pausing to take in the beauty of the universe humbled him. Reminded him that the God who created such a vast cosmos had created him, too. That He was aware of and cared for Cash Herrera.

Herein is love, not that we loved God, but that He loved us, and sent His Son...

Cash shook his head. How had he for so long missed that?

And now, as a father himself, the staggering sacrifice God had made for created beings who didn't love Him hit hard.

If Cash hadn't landed in jail after Lorilee's false accusations, had Deputy Lamar not taken a personal interest in him, would he have remained blind to the truths God painted so clearly in the creation around him? Spelled out in inspired scripture?

"Amazing, Lord," he whispered under his breath, "that You personally care for one lone man standing out here under the stars. A man whose heart is heavy with hope for a lasting relationship with his own son."

A gentle, almost reassuring breeze touched his cheek.

A week ago he'd been waiting to hear if he'd land a job at the Hideaway. He hadn't the slightest inkling that Joey would be hand delivered to his doorstep. A God who could do all that, out of the blue, surely had a plan to make everything work out. Right?

Joey. The new job. The opportunity to make a lasting impact on the future of Hunter's Hideaway so he and his boy could call this place home for a long time.

It was encouraging that Rio agreed to discuss the future of the horse operation. Even though it sometimes seemed she didn't appreciate what she had here at the Hideaway and was intent on getting back to college and a future elsewhere, she had a tender heart. He'd often seen her expression soften the past few days when around Joey. Noticed how she took time to answer his many questions. Gently encouraged him. Teased him to make him smile.

His little Princess had become quite the grown woman.

Cash sighed and again gazed skyward.

"Which is why," he murmured, "I should have turned down her offer to help out with Joey and this horse thing. Kept things strictly business." He shouldn't play with the fire that sometimes sparked between them. He wasn't what a woman like Rio would want for a life partner—and he sure didn't intend on getting sucked into the dizzying vortex of another woman trailed by a pack of lovelorn men—no matter how lonely it got.

Lonely. Is that what he was? Naw. Just solitary. The best place for a man's heart to be if he didn't want it torn apart.

He'd barely stepped onto the front porch of the cabin when his cell phone vibrated. A number he didn't recognize.

"Cash?"

A female. Not Lorilee. As he'd explained to Will, his ex had his number, but when he'd tried hers right after Joey's arrival, it no longer worked.

"Yeah. This is Cash."

"This is Rio." How had he not recognized her voice? He'd have to program her number into his phone since they'd be working together regularly. "I'm sorry to bother you this late. But could I pop over real quick? I just need a few minutes."

She had something to talk about at ten o'clock at night that couldn't be handled over the phone or wait until tomorrow? Weariness washed over him, the stress of the past week finally catching up. "Joey's asleep and I won't be too far behind."

Four fifteen came early these days.

"Okay. Sorry."

He closed his eyes momentarily, rallying his brain cells. *This is your boss calling, bozo.* "I won't be turning in immediately, though. We could meet outside. That won't disturb Joey."

"Are you sure?"

"Totally."

"Okay. I'll be right over."

He shut off his phone and tucked it in his pocket, then sat on the porch railing gazing at the cabins scattered along the trail. Some dark. Others brightly lit. The sound of muffled voices, laughter, carried in the still night air. A country-western rhythm rocked faintly from a distant sound system.

What could Rio possibly want to discuss tonight? And why did the unexpected opportunity to see her set his heart dancing in rhythm with that song he could hear?

He didn't have long to wait. The sound of a vehicle pulling up behind the cabin reached his ears, then she appeared to almost materialize out of the dark and into the pool of the dim front porch light.

Her ponytail swayed entrancingly as she approached, and he couldn't help smiling at the contrast between the tomboy stride of her seven-year-old self and the epitome of femininity heading toward him now.

"Hey, Rio," he said softly as she joined him, conscious of Joey inside. "What's up?"

"I found a few more horse books. I thought I'd drop them off." She slipped a backpack from her shoulder and opened it up. Pulled out three kid-size hardbacks and handed them to him.

"Wow. Thanks, but you didn't need to come clear over here to deliver them." He glanced back at the cabin. "Like I said, Joey's sound asleep."

"I know, but…well, I also wanted to let you know not to spend more of your free time on research and planning for a Hideaway upgrade."

"Why's that?" Had she reconsidered? Decided, as the boss lady, that she didn't want to hear his ideas after all?

"Dad got a call a short while ago from Tallington Associates."

"And?"

"I guess we've been counting our chickens before they're hatched." She gave him a bleak smile. "They changed their mind about Hunter's Hideaway. They're dropping us from their prospects visit schedule. We're out of the running before we even got started."

Chapter Eight

Rio didn't allow herself to linger long after delivering the books and the disappointing news to Cash. What else was there to say? Tallington had offered minimal explanation, so discussion would be pure speculation. Cash probably thought her silly to insist on delivering the update in person. But he was the first person she'd thought of when Dad told her of the change in plans.

Because it affected Cash's future now, too, right?

But for the remainder of the week a pall seemed to settle over the Hideaway. Behind the scenes at least. Not anything that guests would notice. On the surface, it was business as usual. Service with a smile. Nevertheless, despite her family's disparate opinions on the direction of the business, she sensed an underlying letdown in spirits at the lost opportunity.

Except for Cash, who suggested the near miss with Tallington may have been a wakeup call. He drove that theory home on Friday when they arrived at the inn at the same time for a post-trail ride cup of coffee and she felt obligated to ask him to join her.

"Yesterday Luke and your dad went over the horse operation accounts with me." He took a sip from his steaming mug. "We discussed the enterprise finances as a whole."

"Then you can understand why everyone's hopes had risen at the prospect of a steadier stream of bookings from outside our standard customer base."

"I know it's disappointing. But now everyone's looking at the Hideaway with fresh eyes, right? Tallington may not be in the cards, but we shouldn't drop the ball now. We need to be ready for the next opportunity when it arises."

We. He increasingly dropped that word into conversations, a reminder that soon she'd be back in school and he'd be calling the shots here. "That's assuming another opportunity does arise."

He gave a confident nod. "It will. Granted, it may not be dropped in our lap like this last one was. We may have to go looking for it."

"I don't know, Cash…" It wasn't in her nature to be a stick in the mud, but lately everything seemed to take effort, seemed overwhelming. Going back to school, Cash's arrival, the Tallington thing. Even the vow she'd made to God to make something of her life for Him in exchange for an answered prayer weighed more heavily than it ought to.

Running his finger around the rim of his coffee mug, Cash gave her an encouraging look. "I know you're reluctant to move ahead on what we discussed Monday night before that call came in, so I've been hesitant to bring it up. But there's no reason we shouldn't take the lead in rethinking things. Making improvements that will prepare us for the future."

His enthusiasm was almost endearing, but… "There's no rush now, though. We've been given a reprieve. And with our big Memorial Day weekend kickoff starting tomorrow, we're going to have our hands more than full for the rest of the summer."

"And what better time to try out new ideas? Get immediate, real-world feedback. If something doesn't work, we tweak it or replace it entirely with a better alternative. No waiting and wondering and theorizing."

He had a point. And, interestingly, it was becoming increasingly clear that the Hunter clan wouldn't intimidate him once he set his mind to something. He'd hold his own here among the descendants of the hardy Hunter stock of a century ago. Maybe better than she could. She'd, unfortunately, proved to be less confident, less savvy than she'd long pretended to be. Had that changed at all since she'd fled college? Had she grown? Could she trust herself to make good on her vow?

So much was at stake.

"No," he continued, "we won't have much time during the day with things as busy as they'll be, but we can knock out ideas in the evenings, can't we? See if we can get the ball rolling."

She reached for another creamer packet, then tensed as she glimpsed Eliot and his father making their way to the back of the dining room, where staff generally congregated around a trestle table near the kitchen in mealtime shifts.

"Relax, Rio." Cash leaned slightly forward, a twinkle in his eyes. "I don't think either of them will be coming over here to haul me out of my chair because almost a decade and a half ago I cheered my father on in a fistfight. Okay, maybe Eliot would jump at the chance, but not in his father's presence."

She responded with a half-hearted smile.

"I noticed you haven't been joining the other employees for meals this week. That's included in your wage package. It's a good opportunity to get to know people you'll be working with, too."

"But there's no point in making the Greers uncomfortable right off the bat now, is there?" He took another sip of his coffee. "Besides, I try to eat with Joey as often as I can."

Rio again cut a glance at long-time employee Jeb Greer, a big, meaty-around-the-middle man now in his late forties. A dependable guy, he'd worked at the Hideaway in a variety of roles requiring muscle power, which he possessed in spades.

"Thinking back fourteen years," she mused aloud, "it's amazing your father took on a man that size, isn't it?"

Cash's brows lowered as he pushed away his coffee mug. Maybe she shouldn't have reminded him of Hodgson again.

He placed his napkin on the table. "My father didn't always think straight. Wasn't known for good judgment."

"Maybe so, but Jeb was twice his size. And your father *won*."

A faint smile touched Cash's lips. "You think so? He lost his job. Lost the Hunter family's trust. Lost what little respect I had for him once I understood what was going on."

Feeling justifiably chastised, she ducked her head slightly as she downed the last of her coffee. No, Hodgson hadn't won. Far from it.

"So what do you say, Rio?" Catching their waitress as she passed, Cash handed her the leather check holder and shook his head that no change was needed. Then, looking at Rio, he stood and nodded toward the door. "Tallington may be out of the picture, but I don't imagine they're the sole company recommending event sites. Has that been explored in the past?"

Grateful for the change in subject, she stood as well and accompanied him into the inn's lobby. "As far as I know, the Hunters haven't researched outside booking companies before now."

"So there you go. Opportunity awaits." He held open the main door and they stepped outside, then headed to the trail ride office tacked onto the end of the string of adjoining Hideaway buildings. He unlocked the door and they stepped inside a space where riders checked in, secured purses or backpacks, and got fitted for hats, helmets or even boots, if needed.

She slipped behind the waist-high, oak-slabbed counter and booted up the computer. "What exactly do you have in mind?"

She was ashamed she hadn't come up with more definitive ideas of her own, had instead been of a mindset to shoot down whatever he came up with. But that wasn't fair. Not to him. Not to the Hideaway. But she'd had much on her mind lately, especially with her mom's next cancer scan coming up.

Cash bumped one of the boot-fitting benches with his knee to align it with the other one, then straightened boots lining a wall shelf. "I think we're both in agreement—if you're willing to admit it—that the Hideaway is never going to be competition for the upscale dude ranches scattered around the state."

"As I pointed out earlier, that was never our intention." She entered her password and logged into the reservations database. "We don't run cattle, despite Uncle Doug's opinion that adding a few might boost the bottom line."

Cash chuckled as he straightened another pair of

boots, then stepped back to view his handiwork. "As much as I enjoyed working cattle at Cantor Creek, I don't think that's the answer here."

"Of course, it's not. The Hideaway's always been a rustic outpost for hunters of elk, deer, javelina and what have you. An out of the way, deliberately *under-*commercialized setting for horsemen and hikers. It's a haven for outdoor enthusiasts who want to enjoy nature, sit down to a hearty meal among like-minded folks and collapse into a comfortable bed at night."

He glanced over at her. "There you go, then. Don't apologize for what you have here. That rustic element is exactly what we need to play up, not play down."

Unlike her first impression, he was at odds with Uncle Doug's posh plans. She hadn't expected that. "What our guests want is authenticity of experiences, not pseudo-replication of them like at an amusement park."

"You won't hear arguments from me. I mean, when I got up this morning, there were two deer in front of the cabin. I woke Joey up early so he could see them."

"So we both agree—surprise, surprise—that the Hideaway is a specialty niche. That we should play up the outdoorsy element." She leaned her forearms on the counter. "But while I can see how that might translate for things overall, how do we underscore that in the horse operation? I mean, a trail ride is a trail ride, right?"

He moved to the hat racks, where he transferred a misplaced pint-size helmet to the kids' section. "Yes and no."

"Care to elaborate?"

"Well, I think there are a few safety-related factors that need to be addressed around the barns and corrals.

But what we need to reevaluate are our offerings. Starting tomorrow, there will be three standard rides both in the morning and afternoon, switching out the routes so as not to bore the horses or repeat visitors."

"Right." They'd been doing that as long as she could remember. Not a whole lot of hassle.

"So, instead of the same old same old, what if we threw in some variety? Something to entice newcomers—but also to lure back those who've 'been there done that' with us before." He moved to the counter opposite her and, eyes bright with excitement, leaned in on his forearms, too. "Say…a morning breakfast ride? Half-day and full-day rides? Overnight camping? We could offer old-time photography where folks dress up in Western gear to get their mugs taken with a horse. Maybe provide a kid corral birthday party with pony rides, cake and ice cream."

"Whoa, mister. That sounds like a ton of work." Actually, it sounded like a ton of *fun*. But she wouldn't be here for much of it going forward. Would miss out.

"You don't strike me as the kind to be afraid of a little work." Eyes twinkling, Cash tapped her forearm playfully and a tingle zipped up her arm.

"I said it sounds like a *ton* of work." She *did* say that, didn't she? With Cash studying her, that engaging smile playing on his lips, her thoughts were jumbling. "We'd have to rearrange schedules to ensure horse and wrangler availability. Provide adequate supervision for a kids' party. Budget for camping equipment and get Forest Service approvals for the longer rides and overnighters."

He shrugged, not intimidated by her lengthy list of objections.

"And the old-time photography thing?" she said, her

gaze still snagged by his. "While appealing to guests, that could get complicated. Could spook the horses."

"Easy there, girl. Just brainstorming." He brushed his finger along her forearm, and another tingling spark raced across her skin. Although his eyes teased, his soothing tone was akin to the murmurs she'd heard him utter when trying to bridle Wild Card. Gentle. Reassuring. Luring her in...to where he could easily catch the unsuspecting mare.

She stepped abruptly away from the counter.

"We don't have to change it up all at once," he said hurriedly, undoubtedly sensing she was about to bolt. "Trial runs throughout the summer. See what gets a thumbs-up from our guests."

"You've given this considerable thought." But would her family go for it? Approve the funds?

He pushed off the counter as well, but his teasing gaze didn't let up. "So what do you say, *Princess*? Are you up to the challenge?"

To Cash's amazement, she was, despite her initial objections.

And after a crazy busy Memorial Day weekend—the weekly business meeting being moved to Tuesday night to accommodate the holiday—it didn't take a whole lot of persuading on Cash's part to win the family over to budgeting a trial run of a handful of ideas that Rio and he'd agreed on. She jumped in to support his recommendations and together they'd promoted a unified overall "play up what we've got" theme that everyone—except her uncle Doug—bought into with undisguised relief.

For the next three weeks, they reworked schedules, giving the breakfast and half-day rides with a brown-bag lunch a trial run. Those had filled up fast once posted on the website and around the Hideaway. Full days and overnighters were on hold. Birthday parties and photo ops, too. But they were plenty busy anyway.

Somehow, in the midst of it all, Cash found time to work with Wild Card, and without any prompting, Joey even asked Rio to lead him around the corral on Misty a few times, then for daily lessons. So far so good, with both adults having agreed it had to be the youngster's idea all the way.

"Is that one of the projects on the mile-long list you said you had?"

Cash looked up to where Rio had paused to watch him as he crouched to sand a wood railing in one of the corrals at the end of the day. A few weeks ago her comment might have had a disapproving ring to it. But today it merely held a curious note.

"Yep. I imagine I'll be at this kind of stuff throughout the summer. Smoothing rough edges and splinters that could catch on clothing or skin. Wires to clip. Aging boards to replace."

"Good idea, but there's no rush now, so don't push yourself too hard with everything else we have going."

That response was particularly remarkable, if a little unsettling, for they seemed to have fallen into a relatively peaceful routine. Not that they didn't butt heads daily—who'd have thought what was on the breakfast ride menu would prove to be a contentious topic? Or deciding which horses should be allotted for the half-day rides? But for the most part, they were aligned with a mutual goal to expand the Hideaway's horse operation offerings and get things in shape for the next shot at a Tallington-type proposition.

It was a good feeling. But a dangerous one in some respects, at least from his point of view. While as spunky as ever, Rio's gentle side was coming out more and more. Not only with her pregnant mare and Joey, but with *him*, too.

And yet…she didn't trust him.

He swallowed back the bitter taste in his mouth. That truth hit home last night when he and Joey had run out for milk and eggs and a store clerk caught him off guard by talking openly of Elaine Hunter—Rio's mom—having cancer. He wasn't sure what to think of the apparent secrecy, but it had been weighing on his mind. The incident cut deep. Maybe because, if even in a small way after a month at the Hideaway, he was starting to feel like a part of the extended Hunter family. Shouldn't Rio have told him about something that important?

Obviously, that was *his* perception—a foolish one—not hers.

With the sun dipping behind the tops of the pines, she now lingered watching him work as though it was the most natural thing in the world to hang out with him. She wasn't chatting as she often did, though. Something was on her mind, so he wasn't surprised when she finally spoke up.

"You know, Cash, I'm not trying to stick my nose in your business, but have you noticed Joey doesn't talk about his mom?"

He did not want to discuss Lorilee, but since Rio was spending so much time with his son, maybe he shouldn't shut her out entirely. "No, he doesn't."

He gave the fence board an extra hard swipe with the sanding block in his hand. He should have used the cordless sander, rather than going at it with this labor intensive route. But he'd felt the need to apply himself physically, a standby therapy that came in handy when something bothered him, when his patience grew thin.

The nicker of a horse carried from the barn as Rio leaned back against a section of fence beyond where he was working. "You said that until recently he lived with her—not you—from the time he was two. So doesn't, I don't know…doesn't that seem odd to you?"

He'd noticed it, too, and wondered about it. But he hadn't pushed the issue or tried to force Joey into talking other than reminding him that he was available to listen. The kid had his reasons. "When he wants to talk, he'll talk."

"You said she was getting remarried, right? Where is she now?"

"Good question. I've been trying for weeks to track her down when I have time. The two of us have business to tend to regarding Joey."

"At least you have custody."

He rocked back on his heels to look up at her. She might not trust him, but did that mean he shouldn't trust her? "That's the thing. I…*don't* have custody."

Her forehead wrinkled. "But I thought—"

"I don't have *legal* custody. I currently have what you might call possession. His grandma dropped him off with a note from Lorilee, but his mama's cell phone number is no longer a working one, and nobody's inclined to tell me where she and her latest husband have gotten themselves off to."

"So she could turn up tomorrow and take him back?"

"She could." But while he couldn't afford a private investigator, he'd followed Will's advice and retained a lawyer, just in case.

He rose to his feet. Dusted off a pant leg, barely able to disguise a grimace when he glimpsed Eliot Greer climbing into a pickup just beyond the far side of the corral, his disgruntled expression spelling out displeasure at finding Rio in Cash's company.

"So you can see why I don't push my boy to discuss her. Maybe why I'm not trying that hard to find her. I don't think Joey or I want to invite her shadow in on this precious window of time we have together."

An ache in his heart echoed that honest admission.

She nibbled her lower lip. "You sound like you don't think it's permanent."

He gazed up at the puffy clouds overhead now catching the final rays of daylight in a showy display of pinks and purples.

"I hope and pray it is, but until I hold the official piece of paper in my hand..." He shook his head. "Personally, I suspect it won't be long until it hits her that once I have legal custody of Joey, the child support payments stop."

"I imagine that support money would come in handy right now. For Joey's expenses, I mean. Clothes. Food. Babysitter." She pushed away from the fence. "This really helps me understand your situation better."

Didn't she see that there were things he could understand better, too, if she'd come clean with him? Trusted him enough to tell him her mother wasn't well instead of letting him blunder around in the dark and hear it from a grocery store clerk?

He fisted his hand and whacked the side of it soundly against the flat of the fence board. Rio jumped.

"Sorry. I guess I'm more than frustrated right now, with...with the evasiveness of Joey's mother."

"I can see why. But you know, Cash, if money is tight and there are things you need for Joey, my family can—"

"We're good." The wince in her eyes clued him in that he'd spoken too sharply. He gentled his tone. "I appreciate your concern, but I can handle it. This is temporary. I have a friend who's a deputy sheriff doing what he can to locate my ex, so it's only a matter of time before our lawyers get together and hash things out."

He didn't need anyone—especially Rio—feeling sorry for him, thinking he wasn't capable of providing for his boy.

"I need to be patient, which isn't one of my natural gifts." He cracked a smile. "So please don't say anything to your family. This situation is strictly between the two of us."

"Okay. But if there's anything I can do to help..."

"I know where to find you. Thanks."

Her phone chimed, and she pulled it out of her pocket. "Do you mind if I take this? My cousin Garrett and I are playing phone tag."

He shook his head, more than happy to be released from the unwelcome pity he'd detected in her eyes as she moved away to take the call.

Chapter Nine

"So can we count on you, Rio?" Pastor Garrett Mc-Crae's voice held a pleading note as he wrapped up the purpose of his call. "With your personal experience with this kind of thing, I think the kids will listen to you. Parents, too."

"I don't know, Garrett…" Part of her jumped at the chance to speak to the church youth group—and others who wished to join them—following an incident that happened a few days ago right in Hunter Ridge. A seventeen-year-old boy had beat up his sixteen-year-old girlfriend.

But was she ready to go public? To share her story and to attempt to meet the needs of an audience looking for guidance? Even with her recent participation in the spiritual retreat, was she ready for something like this?

"Both kids involved are popular," her cousin continued. "Come from good families. They've occasionally attended our youth group events. It's not like anyone can shrug off what happened and say, 'Well, what can you expect from that part of town or from a family like that?' Dating violence knows no boundaries."

"No, it doesn't." Neither did it know boundaries

within a marriage or—she glanced to where Cash again crouched by the fence in the fading light—postdivorce.

"With your help, though," Garrett urged, "we can get this too-often buried issue out in the open. Start dealing with it at a community level."

Is this what you want for me, Lord? To step out and get a real-life taste of the ministry You're calling me to?

I'm scared.

But how might things have been different if someone had come to her a few years ago and gotten her to see where her relationship with Seth was heading? Helped her to recognize the signs, convinced her she wasn't being paranoid about the little things he'd convinced her were solely in her overactive imagination.

She gripped her phone more tightly. "I'll do it."

"I know this is a big step you might not feel you're ready for. So thanks, Rio." Garrett's voice held a note of pride that confirmed her decision. He'd always been like an extra brother, cheering her on. "Not many know what happened to you in college. You know, why you didn't go back after your freshman year. I think the kids will listen to you."

"I'll do my best."

"And God will do the rest. Guaranteed. Thanks, cuz."

When she shut off the phone, she noticed Cash had come up behind her and now stood a distance away, politely letting her conclude the conversation.

"Everything okay?"

"Yeah." It was. Or it would be once she got over what some might call stage fright. She'd never done much public speaking before, and certainly not about something so personal. "A boy at the high school assaulted his girlfriend, so Garrett's asked me to address the youth group about dating violence."

"Whoa. That's a pretty heavy topic."

"He knows that's where my interests lie—counseling with an emphasis in domestic violence, with a particular interest in reaching young people caught up in destructive dating patterns."

"You mentioned counseling earlier, but I didn't know you'd be specializing in that area."

She slipped her cell phone into her jacket pocket. "I went to NAU two semesters, then circumstances dictated that I step back for a few years. I've been trying to get the rest of my general ed classes out of the way at the junior college in Show Low. I'll launch back into the heart of it again come August."

"Impressive."

She shifted self-consciously, acutely aware of the admiration in his eyes. "I don't know about that, but it's needed. The statistics are alarming. And no race, age, social or economic bracket is exempt. Men, too, can be victims of abusive girlfriends, spouses or other women in their life."

He didn't need to know her personal stake in it, though. Only the academic and theoretical aspects.

A shadow seemed to pass over Cash's eyes. "You won't get arguments from me. Hodgson Herrera was a textbook abuser. Physical and emotional."

A chill raced through her. "He hit you?"

"Some. It was my mother, though, who took the brunt of it. I pulled him off her more times than I care to remember."

She stared at him, her spirits plummeting. *Abusers beget abusers.* You'd think it would be just the opposite, but too often that was the case. Seth, when begging for her forgiveness, had admitted that his own father had used him as a punching bag.

"I had no idea, Cash." Had this been going on right under the Hunter family's nose during the years Hodgson Herrera had worked here? Had her parents known? Grandma Jo? Surely not, or he'd have been jailed long before that altercation with Jeb Greer.

Cash tipped his hat back on his head as the shadows deepened around them. "I kept trying to get her to leave him for her own safety, to get help, but she wouldn't hear of it. Said he wouldn't hit her if she hadn't done something to deserve it. Can you believe that? Sometimes I didn't know who to be the most mad at—Mom or Dad."

A heavy weight settled in her chest. "The victim accepting the blame isn't uncommon."

"He had her convinced that any shortcomings he had were her fault. That her perceptions of what happened were skewed. He had her doubting her own memory, sometimes her sanity."

A prickle of recognition raced through her. "That's called…gaslighting."

His gaze sharpened. "It has a name?"

She nodded. "Where are your folks now? Your mom's not still with him, is she?"

He kicked at the ground. "Dad's in prison. Attempted murder of a guy he worked with. While I don't see or hear from her often, Mom's living with her sister out of state."

He gazed toward a stand of pines on the far side of the corral, a muscle in his jaw working. "But even behind bars with plenty of time to think things over, as far as Dad's concerned it was his crazy wife who pushed him into affairs. He denies any violence directed at her even though I was a witness to it."

He looked back at her, his expression now one of incredulity. "Which is why my ex-wife's claims of violence at my hands, which you've no doubt heard about by now, are so laughable. Yeah, I've decked more than a few men who were asking for it. But hit a woman after what I lived through with my mother? No way."

"But the jury. The judge—"

"My ex-wife can be very convincing and the judge had previously presided in juvie court back when I was a teen with attitude and chronically acquainted with the court system. He knew my track record, but didn't recuse himself. My overworked, court-appointed attorney dropped the ball and didn't make the motions in a timely manner for a new judge, so I got stuck with him. I imagine when sentencing me he thought hitting an ex-wife was one more step in an expected downward spiral, and he'd had enough of seeing my ugly mug in front of his bench."

Was that the truth? Surely there would have had to be strong evidence to lock a man up for six months.

"I'm sorry, Cash." What else could she say? She didn't dare admit that doubts lingered concerning his version of the story. Didn't dare admit she had, if only for a short while, experienced what his mother had experienced. Doubting herself. Blaming herself. Allowing herself to be controlled by a ruthlessly charming manipulator.

But she didn't want Cash—anyone—to pity her. To think her childishly naive. Or stupid. Which was what made the thought of talking to high schoolers at Garrett's request especially intimidating.

Why, though, standing here looking into Cash's expressive eyes, was she longing down deep to believe he *was* telling the truth? Because he *seemed* like a nice guy? Because she enjoyed his company? Because she wanted to believe there were men outside her immediate family who were truly as they portrayed themselves to be? Men of integrity, men with caring hearts. Men who, although by no means perfect, endeavored to live their lives the way God wanted them to.

Was that asking so much?

"I know you're going to believe about me what you choose to believe." He sounded resigned, assuming from her protest regarding the court's decision that she'd made up her mind? "But since we've been talking about family...there's something else I'd like to discuss. Yours."

"Mine?"

He nodded. "Last night when a clerk at the grocery store heard I was working at the Hideaway, working with you, she asked me how your mother was doing. Praised her for her courage in the face of her challenges."

Rio looked into Cash's troubled eyes. Eyes shadowed with unmistakable hurt.

"Why didn't you tell me," he said flatly, "that she has cancer?"

Cash gazed into Rio's startled eyes, searching for answers.

"Do you think keeping it a secret was fair to me?" The resentment in his tone rang clear even to his own ears. "No way would I have let your mom take on the care of Joey had I known. Your whole family probably thinks I'm an insensitive jerk for taking advantage of her like that."

Her eyes widened. "No, that's not true, Cash. She wouldn't have offered if she didn't feel up to it. But she doesn't go around waving her diagnosis and struggles like a flag, and the rest of the family doesn't, either."

"I can understand that, but I was caught off guard last night. Felt like a fool. I pretended I knew what the lady was talking about. Finally got the gist of it and put two and two together." He let out an annoyed huff. "So if you don't mind my asking, how *is* your mother? How serious is this?"

Would she tell him, or was that none of his business, either?

Her gaze drifted almost helplessly around the now-shadowed corral as if seeking the right words, then back to him. "It's serious. Breast cancer."

A muscle in his stomach knotted. "How recent of a diagnosis?"

"She found out right before Luke and Delaney's wedding last Labor Day weekend. She had a single-side mastectomy, then ongoing chemo treatments. Those will be wrapping up by summer's end. God willing."

Rio was leaving in mid-August. Before her mother had concluded treatments?

"She's kept working through all of that? I mean, I've seen her manning the reception desk. I had no idea anything was wrong."

"She's not worked the entire time, just between chemo rounds. She's feeling better now, though, so don't feel guilty about her taking care of Joey. That's something she wanted to do. He brightened her days considerably that week."

"I wish someone would have told me, though. I mean, I care for your mom. I might be considered a newcomer around here, an outsider, but I first met her when I was ten years old. She was good to me when I was a kid."

His memory flashed to the times Rio's mother had stopped to talk to him. Brought him a bottle of water when he'd been helping his dad build fence. Helped him find a lost tool that his father would have likely backhanded him over if not found.

"With you planning to leave the Hideaway, Rio...I never would have guessed this was going on. I'd have thought you'd be sticking close to home where you might be needed."

"I know it might seem strange to you that I'm choosing to head back to college right now, but...I made a vow."

"What kind of vow? To who?"

"To God." She blinked rapidly as if driving back tears.

He hadn't intended to make her cry. "I'm sorry, I—"

"No, it's okay. I want you to understand, so that you don't think I'm abandoning my mom."

"I wouldn't think—" But isn't that exactly what he'd thought? And how often had he concluded that she didn't appreciate her family? He'd have given anything to have had one like hers, but she seemed to take it for granted.

Rio folded her arms almost protectively, like some vulnerable creature of the wild drawing in, shielding itself, and he sensed the falling of night lent her a needed sense of privacy even in the open corral where they stood.

"When Mom was first diagnosed, you can imagine the shock. The helplessness. The fear." She momentarily closed her eyes. "I love my mom, Cash. I can't bear to think of losing her."

"I can understand that."

"Have you ever had a time in your life when you'd do whatever it took to change the course of events that looked inevitable? When you'd vowed to turn your life around and set out on a new direction in exchange for an answered prayer?"

"I have. When I finally realized my life was heading down the wrong road and I turned it over to God three years ago."

"When you were jailed?"

He nodded. "Right before I got out, thanks to months of time and prayer that a deputy sheriff by the name of Will Lamar invested in me."

Her eyes widened slightly. Did she understand what that meant to him? How it impacted his life and would impact Joey's if he could be raised to love the Lord?

"That's sort of what I did, too, except I'd already given my life to Him when I was a teenager. But when Mom…" She blinked rapidly again. "I told God that if He'd spare her life I'd give Him mine for whatever purpose He chose. And I believe that choice, one that had been tugging at my heart for some time but I'd ignored it, is to reach out to young people, to educate and counsel, to make a difference where there's been dating violence or the potential for it."

"And that's why you're leaving the Hideaway now."

Her smile held a tinge of sadness. "My family thinks I've got a burr under my saddle, that I'm doing nothing more than stubbornly stretching my wings. I can't tell them the truth of what's motivating me, though, because they'll try to talk me out of it. But I can't delay, Cash. I can't break my part of the bargain. There's too much at stake."

"Bargain? So you're telling me if you don't do this—don't fulfill this vow of yours—your mom will *die*?"

That sounded more like superstition than faith to him. She was comparing him giving his life to God with this? He hadn't cut a deal with God—he'd never be good enough to earn a relationship with the Creator of the universe. To deserve eternal life. It was a gift.

"Her scans have been clear for months now. Her mother—my grandmother—wasn't so fortunate. She died of breast cancer, so I never got a chance to know her. That fact alone underscores the importance of following through on my vow while there's still time. Who knows if I have that same cancer in my own future? But I believe that ever since I made that promise God's been making a positive difference in my mother's health. So I'm going to uphold my pledge to the best of my abilities."

Cash frowned, struggling to get his head around what she was telling him. "Rio, I don't believe God *bargained* with you for your mom's life. Him choosing to heal her—or not—isn't because you twisted His arm. Cut a deal."

"You make it sound like a bad thing. It's a partnership. A covenant of sorts."

"You're the one who used the word bargain in reference to it. But there's a verse in Psalms where it says that nobody can redeem the life of another person or pay God a ransom for them. No payment is enough. Your vow isn't enough. Your best intentions aren't enough. But it sounds as if you think your mom's life depends on what you do, not on what God chooses to do, His love and grace and mercy."

She clasped her hands and brought them to her heart.

"But He gave me this…this passion, this desire to make a difference."

"I'm not saying He didn't. That doesn't mean, though, that He cut a deal dependent on your performance. What if you do everything you've promised to do and your mom doesn't make it? Does that mean it's your fault? That somehow you didn't perform perfectly? You failed her? Failed God?"

He heard her quick intake of breath. "You're not even trying to understand, Cash."

"I am. You love your mother. You'd willingly sacrifice your own life in exchange for hers. And not being able to do that, you've convinced yourself you've clinched a trade in hopes of sparing her life. Maybe God did call you to this ministry you have in your heart— but I can't buy that following this passion you say you have is the payment He's exacting from you to spare your mom's life."

He looked to her in appeal, praying she'd grasp what he was trying to say. But her expression shuttered, closing him out.

"I shouldn't have told you any of this. I need to stay focused. Follow through. I thought…you'd understand."

"I do. But I don't agree."

"Well, then, I guess there's nothing further for us to discuss, is there?"

"But there's a lot to think about. To pray about, don't you think?" He reached for her, but she stepped back.

Disappointment—in him?—clouded her eyes as she offered a fleeting smile, then moved to let herself out of the corral and walked into the twilight.

Chapter Ten

*C*ash didn't understand.

She'd so desperately needed to share with *someone* the secret she'd kept hidden in her heart since last fall. And when Cash told her of his mother's experiences that were so similar to her own, when he said he'd given his life to God a few years ago, when he said how much he cared for *her* mom, the timing seemed right. An answered prayer.

But he'd misunderstood everything. Had planted doubts in her mind.

I can't buy that following this passion you say you have is the payment He's exacting from you to spare your mom's life.

Who was he to make a judgment like that? But his words troubled her the next few days although neither spoke of it as they teamed up on trail rides, evaluated the new offerings, welcomed Gypsy's daughter into the world and continued Joey's riding lessons. It was evident that the youngster was a born horseman, just like his father.

"Did you and Cash have a falling out?" Her mom, pulling a Sunday breakfast casserole out of the oven as Rio poured the orange juice, glanced inquisitively in her direction.

Caught off guard at the abrupt change in subject—they'd been discussing when her older sisters, Claire and Bekka, might be coming for a visit—she frowned. "What makes you think that?"

"You haven't mentioned him for days, and he's usually a topic of our mealtime conversations."

Had she talked about him that much recently? So much so that when she didn't it was noticeable?

"I wouldn't say we had a falling out." She retrieved the sliced cantaloupe and honeydew from the fridge. "Not exactly, anyway. More like a difference of opinion."

"Not surprising there would be some of that."

"Why?"

"You're both independent, headstrong young people who butted heads as kids. Both like to be boss. But I sense you have an interest in him. True?"

"Who, me?" Interested in a man who'd shot down the sliver of hope for her mother's healing that she'd clung to since last fall? And surely her mother wasn't suggesting a man with Cash's history—despite his denials—as a possible love interest for a daughter who'd gone through what she had.

"I don't hear you denying that your childhood crush may linger on."

Rio laughed as she pulled a spatula from a kitchen drawer. "What crush? Cash and I were foes from the word go."

Mom smiled. "You had the biggest crush on him. Followed him around. Got in his way. Teased and poked and prodded him into noticing you any way you could."

"Reality check here, Mom." She self-consciously rearranged the dishes on the red-and-white-checked tablecloth, aware that her mother was watching her with undisguised amusement. "He locked me in a closet, remember? That traumatized me for weeks. He'd send me off on wild-goose chases to find things for him that didn't exist. Would hide from me. Convinced me, like something out of Tom Sawyer, that cleaning out the slobbery gunk in the bottom of feed buckets was fun and he'd *let* me do his share because I was so special. He made my life miserable."

"And you kept coming back for more. Moped around like a lost puppy for weeks after he and his family left."

"Yeah, right."

"Nevertheless, I stand by my recollections of your childhood years from four to seven."

"What are you two bickering about?" Her father joined them in the kitchen, beelining for the one-cup coffeemaker.

"Mom's having a memory lapse," she teased. "Chemo brain—isn't that what you've been calling it, Mom?"

Her mother shook her head as she set the casserole on a trivet. "Your daughter is in denial. Claims she's never had a crush on Cash."

"Sure she has a crush on him." He fished in a cupboard for his favorite coffee mug. "I think there's more than a bit of the same coming from his direction, too. Grady says he thinks it's making Brax nervous."

"Dad! We're talking about when Cash and I were *kids*."

"Oh?"

"I didn't have a crush on him then, and I don't have a crush on him now."

"Cash this, Cash that." He playfully bumped his wife's arm with his. Gave her a kiss on the cheek. "She always finds a way to wedge him or his kid into the conversation no matter the topic, doesn't she, Elaine?"

"I do not."

"Then you'd better let Anna know you don't want him," Dad teased. "She's smitten, and I'm sure she'd be more than happy to take him off your hands."

Fortunately, Rio's parents mercifully ceased the badgering and they settled into breakfast peaceably enough. She made sure, though, that she didn't mention Cash one single time.

That wasn't easy, considering the measureable progress he was making with Wild Card, the extensive repairs he was overseeing and how well Joey was coming along with Misty. It had been a relief to discover the boy wasn't so much afraid as he was unaccustomed to the big animals. When she'd asked him the first day she met him if he liked horses as much as his dad did, he'd said he didn't know. That had been the truth, not evasion.

They were clearing the table when her dad's cell phone rang. He glanced down at the caller ID and raised a brow.

"Interesting. Must have gotten their time zones confused to be calling this early." People elsewhere always forgot Arizona didn't go on daylight saving time. "But Sunday morning? Guess I'd better take this. See what's up."

With no further explanation, he headed for the French doors and stepped onto the back deck, his voice a hearty welcome. "What may I do for you this fine morning?"

He pulled the doors closed behind him.

Mom gave her an "it beats me" shrug. "Honey, let me clean up here. I know you were wanting to spend time with Gypsy and her foal before church."

It was Cash's turn to oversee things this morning, but she needed to check on Muffin. That's what Joey had named the filly because he'd been eating one when word of her birth reached him. So Rio worked his suggestion into what would become the newcomer's official registered name with the American Quarter Horse Association. Gypsy's Blueberry Muffin.

She'd just arrived at the barn, her thoughts drifting to what Grady had told her mother about Cash's alleged interest in *her*, when Eliot stopped by.

"You're looking mighty fine this morning, Rio."

"Thanks." She'd dodged his attentions in past summers, but he'd been unusually persistent recently. Popping up when she'd least expected it. Complimenting what she was wearing. Doing. Oftentimes lingering longer than she had time for. Like this morning when she needed to check on the mare and foal and get back to the house to get ready for church.

Eliot followed her to Gypsy's stall where she slipped inside, his voice taut. "I want you to know I don't care much for the scheduling changes Herrera's making."

"Why? What's the problem?" Wishing he'd go away, she kept her back to him while grooming the mare. That Eliot would find something to object to when it came to Cash wasn't that surprising.

"That breakfast ride, for one thing. If he wants to head up those, that's his business. But I'd rather sit at a table and down my gravy and biscuits like a civilized human being. Not squat in front of a smoky campfire at the crack of dawn with a bunch of clowns who don't know one end of a horse from the other."

"Come on, now, don't speak of our guests like that, Eliot."

"You know what I mean. If Herrera's so keen on

this sunrise business, he can roll himself out of his nice warm bed and take care of it himself."

"He's doing his fair share on that shift. More than his share. And don't forget, I agreed to the changes, too. We're trying out new things to see what appeals to our clients."

"*Clients?* Is that one of the big fancy words he picked up from that snobby dude ranch I suspect he got fired from? You may not think it's my business, Rio, but that guy is—"

"Standing right behind you," Cash finished evenly, and a startled Eliot spun to face him.

He'd startled her, too.

"Cash," Eliot acknowledged, his tone on the surly side.

"You didn't have to sign on for the breakfast rides. I told you that right from the beginning."

"I heard you. But I didn't want the others feeling stuck with the rooster shift." He said that as if he were protecting them from Cash's poor judgment.

"That's considerate of you, but it's their choice, too. We're running that specialty ride until we determine if folks think it's worthwhile. If the rides don't prove to be popular, don't generate the expected increase in income, then we'll reevaluate. So your input is important and will be taken into consideration like everyone else's."

Covertly watching the two of them as she groomed the tiny foal, Rio couldn't help but admire Cash's handling of the disgruntled man. Her earlier concerns regarding his temper and a possible inability to manage the people side of the horse operation now seemed to be unfounded. As men went, Cash had a lot going for him.

Except that he'd chosen to diminish the promise she'd made to God those many months ago.

With a parting snort Eliot all but stomped off, and she moved to the stall door. "You handled that well."

"Nothing I do makes that man happy, does it?"

"His happiness isn't your responsibility."

"No, but bad attitudes can rub off. I don't want him poisoning the others, making them dissatisfied and thinking we don't have a clue what we're doing." He tilted his head, a faint smile surfacing. "And just for the record, I wasn't fired from the snobby dude ranch. When I landed this job, they graciously waived a two-week notice since trail riding is closed in the heat of summer."

"I didn't think you'd been fired. But Eliot's a black-and-white kind of guy. If you'd have told him from the get-go that the breakfast rides were a done deal, he'd probably not have said much. But by our calling them a test run? He sees that as a sign of weakness, indecisiveness. So he's going to challenge it."

Cash leaned a shoulder against the stall's door frame. "I fully expect the breakfast rides to be a success."

"I agree. I think the fact that the rides are quickly filling up is indicative of that. Don't let someone like Eliot make you question your judgment. You have good instincts, Cash."

He gave her an uncertain smile, no doubt remembering how an earlier conversation had ended when she'd opened her heart to him. Not the greatest of instincts exhibited there, perhaps.

He drew a breath. "Rio, about that night…"

Her phone vibrated and she held up her hand to halt him, pulling the device from her pocket. "My dad."

"Better take it." He stepped back to give her some privacy.

She listened intently to her father, beckoning to Cash

to remain where he was. When the call concluded, she slipped the phone back into her pocket. Then, still stunned at what her father had shared, she turned to Cash.

"You're not going to believe this."

"What's up?"

"Tallington Associates. They've changed their minds and will be coming to evaluate the Hideaway after all. *Five days from now.*"

"Call it quits, Rio." Cash stood in the doorway of the main barn's tack room, where she was almost frantically rearranging bridles and other tack just-so. "It's two in the morning. Nothing we do now is going to make a difference in what happens tomorrow. Or I guess I should say today."

He was tired and edgy himself, but somehow chastising her gave him a sense of control over his own raw nerves.

"I know, but I hadn't noticed until a bit ago that the kids hadn't gotten things put back the way they should have after the last ride today." She pulled a bridle from its wall mount and untangled the reins. "I guess tomorrow's visit has them skittish, too."

"More likely it was the dance in town tonight that occupied their thoughts. They'll have rushed their chores to have time to get cleaned up."

"I forgot about that. While none of them are drinkers, it may be a late night, so we'll have to keep an eye on them come morning. They may not be at their best."

He took the bridle from her hands, acutely conscious of his fingers brushing hers, and hooked it above a saddle. "Give it up, Rio. This is a barn. They're not going to expect it to meet five-star hotel standards."

She looked up at him with weary eyes. "For which I'm thankful. And I'm grateful that your insistence on being proactive about the horse operation helped us also override Uncle Doug's mind-set on the overall direction of the property."

Cash chuckled. "I think he was genuinely disappointed to give up that indoor pool and award-winning chef."

"You can count on it. But while we may not have come close to getting the things done that we'd hoped to, at least we're going into this with our heads held high and knowing genuine hospitality in a rustic setting is a *good* thing."

"The Hideaway has lots going for it. Tallington, if they're a company we want to do business with, will see that."

She stifled a yawn. "Do you think we stand a chance, Cash? Honestly? We're like nothing else they have featured on their website. You noticed that right from the beginning. And although I resented hearing it, that's an important factor."

"It's their loss if they don't recognize the uniqueness of what we offer here. We'll turn right around and find ourselves another interested company. It's a win-win situation."

"I wish I had your confidence." She righted a saddle on a rack. Picked up a dropped hoof pick. Then she stepped back to survey the room.

"Is everything now ordered to suit you?" he teased.

She sighed. "Probably as good as it's going to get, huh?"

"Good. Then I'll walk you to your folks' place and we'll both call it a night."

"Thanks, but you don't need to do that. I have a flashlight on my key chain. I'll be fine."

"I'd normally say suit yourself, but not this time." He motioned to the open tack room door. "After you, pretty lady."

"*Pretty* lady? At this hour? You have quite the imagination." She made a face, but even with that silliness, with strands of matted hair escaping a drooping ponytail and a smudge on her cheek, she looked pretty enough to him.

"Good thing Joey's bunking at Anna's since it's such a late night. Let's get you home and tucked in, too."

"Cash, there's no need for you to—"

She abruptly halted as he folded his arms in an uncompromising stance. Apparently she was too tired to argue any further, for with another sigh she flipped off the tack room light and stepped into the dim aisle between the stalls. Outside they moved off into the trees where the trail became more shadowed. When he reached out to guide her with a light touch to her arm, she pulled away and switched on her flashlight.

While they'd burned the midnight oil side by side the past several days, there hadn't been much time for casual chitchat. They'd certainly not returned to the topic of the vow she'd shared with him, and he figured he'd get his head bit off if he attempted to talk about it anyway. Had he handled that wrong? Should he have let her keep thinking that her mother's healing depended on her ability to keep her promise? He'd wrestled with that for days, knowing she'd expected more of him. That he'd let her down. And that left his heart aching.

They said little as they traversed the trail, skirting around the edge of the darkened main parking lot, now empty except for vehicles belonging to overnight guests.

A few more hours and the sun would rise once again, a new day dawning with Tallington Associates expected on their doorstep early. Was he right in encouraging the Hunters to continue to play up the rustic, woodsy atmosphere of the Hideaway? To emphasize its cabin country heritage that was over a hundred years old? Admittedly, it didn't fit the mold of the other properties Tallington booked for small group events. So would he be way off the mark and today's visit a disappointing disaster the family could lay at his feet?

The tension in his shoulders tightened.

"Something on your mind?" Her words came softly, the crunch of their boots on the trail the only sound in the still night.

He hadn't groaned out loud, had he? "I guess something just hit me like a proverbial ton of bricks."

"What?" He sensed her looking at him curiously, although, like hers, his face would be in shadow.

"Who am I to be advising Hunters on how to present the Hideaway to Tallington? And why did they listen to me? I'm a cowboy whose primary calling card is six months in the county jail and three years working at a dude ranch. Neither of which have a whole lot to do with a place like Hunter's Hideaway."

She poked him in the arm. "They listened to you, cowboy, because you voiced—confirmed—what they believe deep down inside and what Uncle Doug has had them doubting."

"You think?"

"Of course. You gave our signature rustic vibe a legitimate promotional spin. Pushed us beyond the dangers of 'we've always done it this way' to dig deeper and pull out handfuls of gold."

"I did?"

"And you did it when we thought Tallington was a lost cause. Now that they're back in the picture, we're in a position to present ourselves unapologetically. While they may not go for it, like you said, they aren't the lone game in town."

Her words soothed his ragged nerves. The last few days had been intense. Not only his cramming a summer's worth of repair work and painting into a matter of days, but the rest of the family had gotten fired up to freshen the landscaping, top up the crushed rock in the parking lots, clean everything top to bottom, and restain the logs of the main buildings. Grady's artistic, techy wife, Sunshine, had even updated the website to incorporate their newest motto.

Hunter's Hideaway. Where rustic meets relaxing— without apology.

As they entered the little clearing surrounding her family's cabin, he could see that one of Rio's parents had left the porch light on. She stopped and turned to him, her face faintly illuminated by the dim glow.

"Thanks, Cash, for walking me home. I guess I'll see you tomorrow."

"Today."

She smiled. "Right."

He lightly touched her arm. "But before you go, I want to apologize. I know you're disappointed in me. In what I said about the promise you made in exchange for your mother's life."

She held up her hand to halt him. "Cash. Let's not go there. It's late, and I'm not up to discussing this."

He stepped closer and took her hand in his. "I may not agree with you, but I want you to know that I understand how much you love your mother. That you'd—"

"Please, Cash. Don't." Her beautiful upturned face

pleaded, but as their gazes collided, her eyes rounded ever so slightly, her lips parting as if to say more.

But she didn't.

Suddenly dry-mouthed, his gaze dipped to her lips and his heart rate shot up. He should step back. Release her...yet his legs refused to do what his brain was telling them to do.

What would it be like to kiss Riona Hunter? As he stared into her eyes, he was surprised to see a mutual curiosity smoldering there. A longing that matched his own. Her hands tightened on his as she swayed slightly toward him.

She wanted this, too.

What would it hurt? Just this once.

But as he was lowering his mouth to the temptation of hers, she stepped abruptly back, pulling her hands from his.

Shattering the tantalizing moment.

"Good night, Cash."

And then she was gone, leaving him to numbly stand staring after her until the extinguishing of the porch light left him alone in the dark.

Chapter Eleven

What had she been thinking?

She squeezed her eyes tightly shut as she paused in front of Gypsy's stall not many hours later. She couldn't keep letting images of Cash's gaze burning into hers saturate her mind. Fuel her imagination. What was wrong with her? She hardly knew him, yet her heart had breathlessly cried out for him to take her in his arms and...

Cash would be here any minute to prepare for meeting the Tallington representatives. They'd arrived a short while ago, ushered into the inn by her mother, father and Grandma Jo for a high country breakfast. Then it would be Cash's and her turn to convince them that the Hideaway's horse operation was second to none.

But how could she face him when only a few hours ago he'd read her betraying thoughts, been provoked into moving ever closer to gaze down at her with surprise and yearning that equaled hers. And then, as if drawn by the magnet of her will, he'd leaned in...

"Rio?"

At the sound of a voice calling from the far end of the barn, her eyes flew open. Cash.

Fumbling with the latch, she quickly let herself into Gypsy's stall. Had she not learned *anything* from her experience with Seth? To take it s-l-o-w. Be on the alert. Cautiously test the waters. But all she wanted to test last night was how Cash's lips tasted on hers.

She took a steadying breath. "Back here!"

But to her relief he didn't come farther into the barn, remaining just outside the open double doorway. Was he embarrassed, too, at the way she'd practically thrown herself at him? That's why he hung back?

"Grady caught me," he called. "He says your Grandma Jo wants you and me to join the Tallington reps for breakfast. They want to meet the whole family."

Family. Grandma Jo had included Cash in that.

She poked her head out the stall door. "Okay. I'll meet you there. I'm checking on Muffin."

When he departed, she finished up in the barn, then retreated to the inn's restroom to wash up, the tension in her arms evidence that she wasn't looking forward to the day ahead for more reasons than one. As always, she grimaced at the mirrored image, her gaze automatically focusing on her slightly crooked nose—a reminder, compliments of Seth, of the stupidity of her youth.

A reminder, as well, not to make the same mistake again.

When she entered the inn's dining room—the last of the Hunters to arrive—she was introduced to the three events contractor representatives. Elizabeth, a well-dressed middle-aged woman—or at least well dressed for Boston business, not a mountain country Arizona excursion—seemed unexpectedly approving of the breakfast special, complete with scrambled eggs topped with fresh salsa, sausage, seasoned potatoes, rosemary–pine nut banana bread and prickly pear jelly.

Jim, a friendly gentleman in his early fifties who quizzed them on the Hideaway's history, documenting in a leather-bound journal their responses and his own impressions, looked comfortable in slacks and a golf shirt.

And Edmund, an eager-looking man in his early thirties, boasted obviously new jeans, boots and a bright plaid collared shirt. A red bandanna looped around his neck, and, undoubtedly, a treasured cowboy hat must be secured on a horseshoe hook by the door. He expressed disappointment at having missed the breakfast ride. But although his enthusiasm and somewhat gaudy attire might lead one to dismiss the role he played in this critical visit, she recognized a razor-sharp intelligence and observance of detail.

Cash caught that, too.

"He's the one who won't let anyone pull anything over on them," he said after breakfast as they headed to the trail ride office to await their turn to be interviewed and show their guests around the horse facilities. "I have a feeling not much gets by that guy."

Although Rio couldn't bring herself to look at Cash during the breakfast meeting, there hadn't been a single moment that she'd been unaware of him. Now, as they awaited the Tallington reps, she resorted to fleeting glances as they lingered outside the office, enjoying the cool summer morning that set off this part of Arizona from the lower elevations. They couldn't ask for better weather for showcasing the Hideaway.

"Elizabeth," she managed, darting a look in his direction despite the embarrassment of their previous encounter that still gripped her, "seemed to appreciate the antiques in the dining room and lobby. I think she'll like that in the guest rooms at the inn, as well. The cabins, too."

Rio needn't have worried about carrying on a conversation with him, though, for there were people coming in for a morning meal to greet and others to welcome back from the breakfast ride. Then soon enough the two Tallington males exited the inn with a forty-minute trail ride at the top of their agenda, Elizabeth having preferred to remain inside to tour the inn's kitchen, conference rooms and guest accommodations.

All went well, even when Edmund inserted his foot too far into the stirrup and got himself hung up. King had been a good choice for his mount, a showy-looking appaloosa gelding that would appeal to the young man's flashy tastes but nevertheless had an award-winning disposition and limitless patience.

Afterward, the two accompanied Rio and Cash on a tour of the horse facilities, grilling their hosts on daily routines, sanitation and safety measures. Staff experience, quality and training of horses, maintenance of equipment and insurance coverage figured in, as well.

She later saw them talking to guests who'd come back from a ride. Nice enough folks, but highly focused. Even the overeager Edmund wasn't given to idle chitchat once they got down to serious business. They offered no comments as to whether they liked or disliked something, Jim jotting furiously in his journal.

When several hours later the two reps returned to the inn to join Elizabeth, Grandma Jo and Rio's parents for a lunch meeting, Rio reluctantly approached Cash, who was inside the barn checking out King's tack, inspecting the stirrups with a keen eye.

"Do you think," he said from where he'd placed the

saddle on a bale of straw, "that Edmund deliberately stuck his foot through this stirrup? He had heeled boots on. It would take effort to do what he managed to do."

"You mean maybe he deliberately did it to test how King would react and what we'd do? Kinda risky, though. Good way to get yourself dragged down the road should a horse spook."

"I could be wrong, but despite his dudish mistakes, I think the man knows horses."

Which made her all the more uneasy that they'd possibly been evaluated by a professional horseman.

With Cash acting no differently around her than usual, though, she garnered courage for a question that was gnawing at her. "So how do you think things are going? Overall, I mean."

He lifted the saddle. "No telling."

Although in the week hours of the morning he'd expressed doubts that promoting the rustic elements of the Hideaway was the best way to go, she'd hoped he'd be upbeat today. Set her fears to rest.

Saddle propped on his hip, Cash paused on his way to the tack room to look back at her, almost as if sensing her disquiet. "We run a safe and well-organized operation, Rio. Are inspected regularly. I don't know what more they could want."

Then he moved on and, with a sigh, she headed to her folks' cabin to make herself a sandwich and go over her notes for that evening's talk with the high school youth group. She'd again wrestled in the night with Cash's take on her vow, and the merit of his words had her seriously questioning that perhaps she'd missed the intention of what she'd thought God had spoken to her.

And did Cash turning his life around, giving himself to God, mean that she no longer had reason to fear him?

That possibility sent hope bubbling that she quickly tamped down. She didn't dare get ahead of herself. It wasn't uncommon, she'd heard, for those incarcerated to "come to Jesus" in hopes of shortening their sentences, yet abandon Him later.

Only time would tell.

She'd finished lunch, readying to return to the barn, when an agitated Grady barged in to report the departure of the three Tallington representatives.

Barely a half day? Six hours?

That couldn't be good.

With a sickish feeling in the pit of her stomach, she commandeered Grady and took off to give Cash the news.

"Lookin' good, Cash."

Luke gazed up the ladder to where Cash was finishing another coat of paint on the back of one of the barns with a flourishing sweep of the spray gun.

"Everything always takes more time than you think it will, doesn't it? I'd hoped we could have this second coat done before the Tallington visit."

"It's done now, though. You and Rio have been kicking major fanny out here. These barns look great. I hope those reps recognize the work that's been put into the horse operation." He glanced around. "Where is Rio, anyway?"

"Haven't seen her since lunchtime." He thought she might join him to finish up the painting before their next trail ride. But clearly, after the near-miss kiss he'd almost pulled off last night—misinterpreting all the signals like some overeager teenager—she was steering as far from him as she could get today. She could barely bring herself to look at him.

That fact left Cash a little uneasy with Luke's unexpected visit to check the painting progress. During one of those Sunday dinners when Cash had joined the family, there had been plenty of laughter when Grady and Luke bandied about those classic "so you think you want to date my sister" jokes. Apparently they had a reputation as Rio's personal guard dogs.

Did they have a radar that detected when a male was getting too close?

"I heard your kid's coming right along with his pony."

"Not too bad considering he's a late bloomer. I think it's Rio working with him that's made a big difference."

Luke angled a look at him. "Everything okay between you two?"

"Joey and me?" What was this, an experienced father of three here to offer advice? Had Rio told her family about his financial situation even though he'd asked her not to? About his struggles with parenting Joey?

"Actually..." He studied Cash. "I was referring to you and Rio. I'd kind of gotten used to the way you two seemed to be hitting it off. To the way this summer she's come out of the shell she'd curled into when she came back from college. I'd put that partially down to the time she's spent with you and your boy. But in the past week or so, she's pulled back in again."

Luke's eyes narrowed as if expecting a full confession of wrongdoing. But Cash wasn't at liberty to discuss what had come between them—differing views on Rio's vow.

"I wouldn't worry too much about it, Luke. She has a lot on her mind. School. Turning things over to me. Then this Tallington visit has added pressure. We're all feeling it."

"Could be." Luke nodded, not appearing satisfied with Cash's explanation. "But keep an eye on her for me, will you? Something's up there. I'm just not sure what."

If Cash wasn't mistaken, Luke was about to say more when Rio and Grady rounded the side of the barn. And if the look on their faces was any indication, they weren't here to share good news.

Cash climbed down a few steps on the ladder, then leaped to the ground. Placed the painting equipment at his feet.

"Well, folks." Grady's smile was grim. "Hate to be the bearer of bad tidings, but we crashed and burned."

With a sinking feeling, Cash exchanged a look with Luke. That wasn't what any of them wanted to hear. Not after he'd encouraged the Hunters to present the rustic Hideaway to their visitors *without apology.*

"They turned the Hideaway down flat?" He hadn't expected anything like that. At least not so quickly.

Grady shrugged. "Not officially. May as well have, though. They said someone would get back to us. But how else can you interpret it when they only hung around not much more than a handful of hours? Uncle Doug's about to blow a gasket."

Luke set his hands on his hips. "You're telling me they're gone? Already?"

"Right after lunch." Rio turned somber eyes on her brother. "They didn't stay for a moonlit hayride. Or spend the night in the cabins we'd reserved for them."

"That doesn't sound good." Luke wearily rubbed the back of his neck. "Personally, though, as much as I hate to see this opportunity slip through our fingers, as much hard work as all of us put into it, I'm glad to have this behind us regardless of the way things have turned out. It's been hanging over our heads since the middle of May. But this isn't the end of the world."

"No, it's not." Cash leaned a hand against the ladder. "I'm still optimistic."

Grady cut him a doubtful look. "Glad someone is."

"I'm serious. They were here for over half a day. Toured the cabins, rooms and meeting spaces. Seemed to enjoy breakfast. They rode horses and got a good look at the surrounding forest. The views."

"Then they hit the road without a word of encouragement," Rio flatly concluded. "Sounds like they were real impressed."

He gazed at the semicircle of cheerless faces. "Look, they covered a lot of territory in a short time, right? I don't know that a moonlit ride, another meal or spending the night here would have swayed them one way or another if they didn't like what they'd already seen."

"But that hayride is fun," Rio defended. "And who wouldn't want to stay overnight and check out the quality of the service? The evening meal?"

"These people are viewing a lot of properties this summer." Until Tallington gave them a flat-out no, as far as he was concerned the game was still on. "They've probably seen quite a few already. They know what they're looking for and how to spot it. I didn't get the impression that this was a first time out for any of them. There's still hope. Plenty of it."

"Well, think what you want, Cash, but I'm not holding my breath." Luke again rubbed his neck. "And I, for one, am calling it a day."

Cash folded his arms. "Still no shut-eye?"

Luke gave him a puzzled look, then laughed. "Not much. My first kiddos were flatland born, but I've heard babies often come early at these higher elevations. It's not panning out that way, though, and I think Delaney's ready for me to drive her up to the top of the over twelve-and-a-half-thousand-foot San Francisco Peaks to see if we can get things moving."

Everyone laughed, the tension from the bad news dissipating somewhat. After a few more minutes of commiseration, Grady and Luke headed off.

But Rio lingered. "Don't blame yourself for this, Cash."

He focused on collapsing the extension ladder. "They may be drawing up a contract as we speak."

"You don't really believe that, do you?"

"It's as easy to believe as not to. And feels a whole lot better."

"What I'm feeling is let down." She turned glum eyes on the freshly painted barn. "We worked so hard. All of us. We really needed this."

"Everything works for the good," he reminded her. "Don't give up yet."

She remained silent, staring at the barn, then looked back at him. "What was Luke talking to you about before Grady and I showed up? It wasn't about Tallington's departure, because neither of you knew about that yet."

"He was asking about you, actually."

She scoffed. "That sounds ominous."

"He didn't think you seemed like yourself this past week and wanted to make sure everything was okay with you."

With an unladylike snort, she pinned him with a skeptical look. "And he asked *you*? What did you tell him?"

"That you had a lot on your plate and a lot on your mind." He studied her a moment. "Was I off the mark?"

"Right on target."

"Tonight's that thing you're speaking at, right? The youth group talk on dating violence."

She looked surprised he'd remembered. "Right."

"Nervous?"

"It shows?"

"If you need some moral support, I'd be happy to go along."

Alarm flickered through her eyes. Okay, guess that wasn't a good idea.

"Thanks, but that would make me even more nervous. I told Garrett I actually hope it won't be that big of a group. That it's mostly high schoolers and not a bunch of adults. I asked my family not to come—except for Luke's teens, Anna and Travis, of course."

"I'll be praying, then. What you're doing is commendable. Anything that might prevent young people from falling into the destructive patterns I grew up with is worthwhile."

He'd sure like to be there, though. To let her know what mattered to her mattered to him.

But when exactly, had he stopped building walls around his heart? Stopped comparing her to Lorilee?

In the empty hallway where she paused to pray, voices of a growing crowd of young people carried back to her from the auditorium of Christ's Church of Hunter Ridge.

She wiped the light sweat from her palms onto her jeans, thankful Cash hadn't accompanied her. She wasn't ready for him to know what happened to her. He'd be angry with her, just like he was angry with his mother for allowing herself to be trapped in the relationship with his father. She wasn't ready, either, for him to know she'd given his concerns about her vow prayerful thought. Was seeing it with fresh eyes.

Tension knotted in her upper arms.

This was it. In a matter of minutes she'd stand in front of those who might be quick to judge. Who might believe her to have been naive. Immature. Stupid. Deserving of whatever Seth had chosen to deliver.

Maybe she'd been all of those, except the latter.

Mostly, though, she'd been a girl in her late teens who'd longed to love a man and be loved in return—and got it all wrong. Not because her motives were amiss, but because some people took advantage of others. Thought only of themselves.

She glanced at the open door to the auditorium, grateful for these moments to reflect on the two high schoolers whose heartbreaking circumstances initiated this gathering. To consider how she might best communicate what needed to be said. Heard. Understood.

Would things have been different for her if Luke and Grady hadn't been so protective, thinking none of the boys she crushed on were good enough for their little sister? Word got around that if you wanted to go out with Rio Hunter, you'd run the big brother gauntlet on a first—and what would probably be your only—date.

Maybe if her brothers hadn't made themselves such a nuisance, she'd have been better equipped to handle her first serious relationship. Would have had more boy-girl experience and been a better judge of men.

But in reality, she couldn't blame her brothers. And for too long she'd blamed herself.

Garrett poked his head into the shadowed hallway. "Ready, Rio?"

"Ready as I'll ever be."

Her cousin must have sensed something in her voice,

for he stepped into the hallway and closed the door behind him. Held open his arms to her. "Come here, gal."

Without hesitation, she went straight to him, absorbing the strength of this man who knew God—and her—so well.

"Are you going to be okay?" he whispered.

She nodded.

"You don't have to do this."

She gave him a hug. "But I do, Garrett."

"You're sure?"

She closed her eyes for a moment, as the words that had haunted her for days echoed through her mind. *I can't buy that following this passion you say you have is the payment He's exacting from you to spare your mom's life.*

She stepped back and smiled at Garrett. "Yes, I'm sure."

And she was.

Not because she had to do this so God wouldn't snatch her mother away. No, God loved her mom more than she did. Her healing didn't depend on her daughter's perfect performance.

Rather, she was doing this because she desperately wanted young people to know they were valued by Someone whose deep love for them went far beyond that of any boyfriend or girlfriend they would ever have. That they, too, deserved to be treated by others like a daughter or son of God Most High.

But as Garrett ushered her into the auditorium…it hit her. She would be doing this for all the wrong reasons if it weren't for Cash. She'd been wrong not to invite him to join her.

He *should* be here tonight.

Chapter Twelve

If only he could get up the nerve to ask Rio out. Maybe find a way to bridge the distance that stretched between them despite what he sensed was a mutual attraction.

That was a crazy thing to be thinking, especially right now. With the Hunter clan and their longtime friends as thick as fleas on the back patio of the Hideaway, Josephine Hunter's early Sunday afternoon birthday party was in full rockin' swing. Her beautiful blonde granddaughter was handing out ice-cream bars, surrounded by kids of all ages—including *his* son, who seemed to think he had every right to line up with the Hunter offspring.

Standing off to one side, a cup of soda in hand, Cash was grateful to be included in the Sunday afternoon event honoring the family matriarch. But unlike Joey, he didn't feel as though he belonged there, was one of them. Instead, he was deeply aware that even though he'd been here since late May—it was July now—and had been every bit a major contributor in the push to win Tallington as any of the Hunters, he was still an outsider. Would always be one—even when he stepped into the horse operation management role next month.

He hadn't asked a woman out since his release from jail, although there had been plenty of opportunities. Nice, attractive women. But knowing the role he'd played in his failed marriage, as well as still dealing with Lorilee's infidelity, didn't leave him with a whole lot of confidence to try again. So why had he gotten it into his head that a woman like Rio might be persuaded to take an interest in one of the Hideaway's hired hands?

"Need a refill there, Cash?" Delaney sidled up next to him, looking for all the world as if she'd rather be anywhere but here—with top pick being the regional hospital's delivery room.

He shook his ice-filled cup, sloshing the carbonated beverage. "Thanks, but I'm good."

"Hunters know how to throw a party, don't they?"

She scanned a crowd that looked to be having a better than good time. A better time than he was having here on the sidelines.

"Great turnout to honor Jo."

"She deserves it." Silent for a moment, Delaney tilted her head curiously. "You going to the rodeo tonight?"

This was the final evening of a three-day event held at the High Country Equine Center in Canyon Springs, about thirty minutes from Hunter Ridge. "Been thinking about it."

"Grady and Sunshine are going. Take Rio."

Did Delaney have a hotline to his brain? His gaze slid involuntarily to the smiling blonde handing out the last of the frozen treats.

"I'm serious," Rio's sister-in-law continued when he didn't immediately respond. "She needs to get out more."

At that moment, Dave Hunter, standing at a round table next to his seated mother, firmly tapped a spoon on his empty tea glass. The sharp, insistent ring echoed across the patio.

"Looks like my dad's going to launch into speech time. I'd better find Luke and Chloe." Delaney slipped away into the crowd, and Cash set his soda down on a nearby picnic table to focus on Rio's father.

"May I have your attention, please?"

The crowd quieted in anticipation of what the man gazing fondly at his mother was about to say. Although smiling, Jo was firmly shaking her head, her steady gaze, if Cash wasn't mistaken, issuing her son a warning.

"She wants him to keep it short and not real mushy," Rio confided as she appeared at his side, holding out an ice-cream bar.

"What's this?" he whispered.

"What's it look like? Eat it before it melts."

She pushed it into his hands, but he didn't want to eat the thing right now. He looked around helplessly until he spotted a kid nearby and handed it off to him.

"Today we're here," Dave began, "to celebrate Jo Hunter's birthday, and we thank all of you for coming to honor this amazing woman."

The crowd clapped as Dave and his mother exchanged a smile.

"As you know," he continued, "we—"

"Hold on! Hold on! Special delivery." The crowd parted as, from behind them, a rotund man hurried into their midst, carefully carrying one of the biggest vases of red roses that Cash had ever seen.

"Bill Stanley, part-time florist at the local grocery store," Rio whispered. "Look at the size of that thing."

"He must have raided every floral shop within a sixty-mile radius."

Happiness lit Rio's face. "I imagine they're from the family."

With a flourish, the grinning deliveryman carefully placed the massive vase on the table in front of the astonished birthday girl. Unable to suppress a smile, Jo stood to inspect them, leaning in to drink in their rich scent.

"Thank you. These are beautiful." She gave her offspring a look of mild reprimand, undoubtedly aware of how much those dozens of roses had cost. "You've outdone yourselves for this old lady."

Dave frowned and leaned over to say something to Elaine, who shook her head. Then he raised his eyebrows at his sister Suzy and brother Doug, who also shook their heads.

"Um, Mom." Dave nodded at the flowers. "Maybe you'd better read the card."

With an indulgent smile, she retrieved an envelope from the arrangement and pulled out the card. Then, drawing her reading glasses from her pocket, she slipped them on, cleared her throat and read aloud.

"'Congratulations, Mrs. Hunter.'" She paused, dipping her head slightly to look over the top of her glasses at her offspring gathered around the table. "*Mrs. Hunter?* After all these years it's entirely acceptable to call me 'Mom.'"

The crowd laughed.

"'Congratulations, Mrs. Hunter,'" she repeated, then gave a dramatic sigh. "'Thank you for your recent…'" Frowning, her voice drifted off as she read silently. Then she placed her hand to her heart. "Oh, my. A happy birthday to me, indeed."

"What's it say?" Doug loudly demanded.

She shook her head, obviously overwhelmed. Then,

with everyone watching with bated breath, she again held up the card, the strength in her voice belying her eighty-some years. "'Thank you for your recent hospitality. We look forward to working with you and your fine family for many years to come as Hunter's Hideaway joins the Tallington Associates lineup of superior special events venues. We'll be in touch, soon.'"

Rio gasped, gripping Cash's arm.

"And it's signed," Jo continued, still looking dazed, "Elizabeth, Jim and Edmund."

For a moment, people around them glanced uncertainly at each other, those outside the family in particular not understanding the significance of what had just been read.

Then across the way, Grady suddenly let out a rip-roaring whoop. "Tallington! They're taking us on!"

A cheer went up from the Hunters scattered throughout the crowd. Whoops. Whistles. Back pounding. And like a house on fire, word spread as to the meaning of the card's message, setting off another wave of cheers and applause.

"I can't believe this." Rio stared up at Cash.

Dumbfounded himself, he gazed down into her beautiful sparkling eyes. "Believe it!"

Laughing, she abruptly threw her arms around his neck and hung on for dear life. "We did it, Cash, we did it!"

Their "without apology" approach had won over Tallington.

"We sure did." He wasn't quite sure what to do with her hanging on to him like that, but with everyone else around them reacting similarly to the unexpected news, he tentatively allowed himself to rest his hands on her waist.

She gave him another hearty squeeze. "Looks like we showed Uncle Doug, didn't we? He's going to have to eat his words."

Cash doubted he'd live to see that day. But this opportunity to hold Rio close was reward enough, and caught up in the moment, he garnered the courage to return her hug.

Still laughing and shaking her head in disbelief, she drew back slightly to look up at him. His heart kicked into overdrive, his mouth suddenly dry at the reality of her warm, slender body wrapped in his arms. This was right. So right. Did she feel it, too? But gazing into her eyes, he recognized at once the moment when she became aware of how close they stood to each other. How she'd thrown herself into his arms. How his arms had wrapped around her, pressing her close to his heart.

That awareness motivated her to slowly pull away, blushing furiously. He wasn't ready for the moment to end and, taking her hands in his, he couldn't help but blurt out what had been on his mind all day. "Let's go someplace and celebrate tonight. Kick up our heels."

She looked confused, apparently not understanding what he was asking of her. That he was asking her out. But he pushed ahead, not letting the uncertainty in her eyes hold him back.

"I can't think of a better way to celebrate an event like this than hitting the rodeo in Canyon Springs. How about it?"

"You mean—like the two of us?"

"Yeah, sure. Why not?"

"A date?"

His hopes rose, despite the ebbing of the sparkle in her eyes. "I'm not opposed to calling it that if you aren't."

"I don't know, Cash…"

"Sunshine and Grady are going." Why'd he say that? As if his original intent was a group outing. But if she'd go, knowing they'd be there, too, well, so be it. He'd take whatever he could get.

"It sounds like fun. I haven't been to a rodeo in ages, but—" She slipped her hands from his. "I'm not sure…"

"About what?"

"Well, I'm going to be leaving Hunter Ridge next month…"

Okay. Here it comes. The breath he'd been holding slowly escaped his lungs, deflating right along with his hopes. She was about to deliver the let-him-down-gently routine he'd been on the receiving end of a few times before. Though not often, he was relieved to say.

"So it's probably not," she continued, "a good idea for us to—"

"You don't need to spell it out, Rio. I get it."

But before either could say anything more, Rio's smiling parents hurried up to them, arms wide with celebratory hugs. Soon, her Grandma Jo and other Hunters joined them.

He stepped back out of the family circle that, as a boy, he'd dreamed of being part of. And when it appeared he'd been forgotten, he slipped away to find Joey.

Hoping to end the day on a more positive note with his son, he nevertheless couldn't turn him down when he begged to play with his friends and spend the night with Luke and Delaney's family. Which explained how Cash ended up back at his cabin all alone, tune after tune of lost-love country-western songs playing mournfully on his radio.

No TV. Nothing he wanted to do on his laptop. He did try reading for a while, but eventually found himself standing at a sink full of still-soaking breakfast dishes, his mind wandering to those too-short moments when he'd held Rio in his arms, then watched woodenly as she struggled to turn him down without hurting his feelings.

An unsuccessful effort.

"Well, that was fun, Lord," he mumbled as he washed the dishes. He should have left well enough alone, just accepted it for what it was. Not tried to turn that celebratory event into something more.

How'd he get so clueless about women? Or maybe he'd always been.

The cabin door rattled under a firm knock, and he groaned under his breath. He didn't need company. But with the radio blaring and the clatter of dishes in the sink carrying through the open windows, he was a sitting duck.

Having dried his hands, he turned off the radio.

Then with a burst of resigned willpower, he opened the door. And his heart stilled.

Rio.

"If the invitation still stands…" Her eyes searched his, an uncertain smile touching her lips. "I'd like to go to the rodeo with you."

"You look like you're having fun." Cash winked at Rio as they walked along the shadowed, tree-lined lane outside the High Country Equine Center. When the kids' calf riding started, he'd said they should step out of the crowded arena for a breath of fresh air. And a few moments in private under the star-filled sky, perhaps? Her heart fluttered in anticipation.

And to think she'd almost missed out on this. The drive to Canyon Springs. Window shopping along Main Street when, to her surprise, he held her hand. Laughing at the puppies in the pet shop window. Sitting side-by-side in their reserved seats, arms occasionally brushing as rodeo events unfolded before them.

It had been a close call. At the moment of Cash's invitation, she'd mechanically withdrawn into the protective shell she'd lived in since the day Seth had hit her. But, in spite of the milling crowd, a keen-eyed Grandma Jo had witnessed her customary retreat and called her out on it. Encouraged her to follow her heart.

"I'm having *tons* of fun." She smiled up at Cash. "Hanging out at a rodeo with a good-looking cowboy, how could I not?"

He glanced around them. "You're here with a *good-looking* guy? Maybe I'd better get lost. I don't want to cut in on some other man's territory."

"Oh, you." She laughed and cuffed him playfully on the arm. Grandma was right. Cash had entered into a relationship with God, had turned his life around and was building a new track record. She no longer had to be afraid.

For a long moment their smiling gazes held.

"We made a good team meeting that Tallington deadline, didn't we, Cash?"

"We did. We've come a long way, haven't we? From your being a childhood pest who plagued me to partnering on something that will make a difference to Hunter's Hideaway for a long time to come."

She pretended offense. "Pest?"

"You know you were."

"Mom and Dad think I had a crush on you." Now why did she bring that up?

He chuckled. "You had an interesting way of showing it."

"A girl can't wear her heart on her sleeve, you know."

She didn't attempt to hide a flirtatious smile. "It puts her at a disadvantage."

He pursed his lips thoughtfully. "Even at such a young age, girls think about stuff like that?"

"Subconsciously, I suppose. Survival instinct."

"Interesting." He gave her a sidelong glance. "You females are complicated creatures, aren't you?"

"Mmm-hmm. Keeps men on their toes."

"You certainly keep me on mine."

"Do I?"

"Always."

Again their gazes held, and when his dipped briefly to her mouth, her heartbeat sped up as the remembrance of that earlier near-miss kiss flashed through her.

She looked back at the brightly lit facility. A round of applause echoed in the night. "Well, I guess we'd better get inside for the remaining events. We don't want to miss the fireworks of the bull-riding finale."

He took a step closer, his gaze intent in the dim light. "Unless I'm mistaken, we could spark a few fireworks of our own right here and now."

She sucked in a sharp breath.

"Agreed?"

Her eyes locked with his, she slowly nodded.

His hand now resting on her waist, he leaned in, his eyes searching hers. She could feel his heart beating under the hand she pressed to his rock-solid chest to keep from swaying toward him.

And yet he waited, his mouth hovering inches from hers.

"What's the hold up, cowboy?" The words came out in a breathless squeak and her face heated. Thankfully in the dim light he wouldn't see that blush.

The corners of his mouth curved upward. "You have

no idea, do you, Rio, how beautiful you are? How special you are. What a difference you've made in my life and the life of my son in such a short time."

How should she respond to that? *Thank you? Happy to oblige.* Or—she drew a shaky breath—*Hurry it up, mister, before I pass out waiting for you to make your move.* Why was he deliberately torturing her like this?

And then. Finally. He closed his eyes and leaned in again.

A lightning-powerful jolt bolted through her when his lips made tentative contact with hers. And when she didn't pull back, they pressed in warmly with increased confidence. She responded, fully engaged in an amazing moment she'd only dreamed of. *Could this guy ever kiss!* The faint scent of his aftershave and the roughness of his five-o'clock shadow under her fingertips sent her senses reeling.

She hadn't let a man kiss her since…

No. She squeezed her eyes more tightly shut, refusing to allow the past to intrude on the present. Allowing herself to sink into his arms, she responded to his kisses as if God had intended this all along.

Had He?

As the tender moments stretched, leaving her almost light-headed, that possibility sent hope curling through her heart. Was this the love she'd longed for since she was a teenager?

When Cash drew back—all too soon—she reluctantly allowed him to. But her heart cried out *Encore! Encore!* She didn't want the romantic moment to end.

His eyes twinkling, a smile quirked. "You sure know how to let a man know his attentions are welcome."

Her face warmed. Had she gotten carried away?

Made a fool of herself? "Too hot for you to handle, eh, cowboy?"

There, that set the right tone. Took control again.

He laughed as he stepped back, glancing around as though suddenly aware of their public surroundings.

She poked him in the chest. "Kinda late to be checking for an audience, don't you think?"

He grinned. "So what do you say to heading back inside and grabbing an ice-cream cone before the final events?"

He'd kissed her almost senseless and his response was to now offer an ice-cream cone like she was still only seven years old? He was satisfied that she was good with that?

"We could, I suppose."

"Was there something else you wanted to do? Take a look at the tack and trailer displays again? See what time that country band will be tuning up?"

Men. She shrugged and stepped around him, heading purposefully toward the equine center.

"Whoa, Rio." He caught up with her and snagged her arm, drawing her to a halt. "What's going on?"

"In case you've forgotten, some guy took it upon himself to kiss me like nobody's business. Now he's acting as though he just clicked his remote to another channel midgame."

In the brighter light closer to the building, she didn't miss the speculative gleam in his eye.

"That's what you think, is it?"

"Sure seems like it. I may just track down Grady and Sunshine and sit out the rest of the evening with them."

Laughing, he grabbed her hand. "Oh, no, you don't, pretty lady."

Sweeping his arm possessively around her, he tipped

her slightly back. Then his mouth came down on hers again. No lingering this time. Straight to the purpose on which he'd set his mind.

Once more, her insides melted as his lips caressed hers. *Cash.* Coherent thought faded at the amazing way it felt to be held in his embrace. But before she could loop her arms around his neck to pull him closer, he jerked violently away.

Or rather he was pulled roughly from her by a shadowy figure behind him.

"Just like your old man, eh, Herrera? Can't keep your hands off what doesn't belong to you."

Even standing several feet away from him, Rio could smell the alcohol on Eliot's breath. But before either could react to his intrusion, the bigger man doubled up his fist and plowed it into Cash's jaw, sending him staggering.

Her scream was overridden by the roar of the crowd from the arena stands. "Eliot! No!"

But in a flash, eyes heated with rage, Cash regained his balance and rushed forward, his fists firing back with the accuracy of a heat-seeking missile. One slammed into Eliot's stomach and, as the man doubled over, the other followed up at lightning speed with an upswing blow to his jaw.

With a groan, Eliot sank to his knees.

Chapter Thirteen

Without thinking, Cash had instinctively reacted. Now, Rio's muffled scream echoing in his ears, his attention was diverted from the man at his feet to the woman whose eyes were wide with horror.

His hands still clenched, she was staring at him—not at Eliot—with a look that made his blood run cold.

"Don't, Cash. Please, don't."

Then she turned and ran.

Dazed—one moment holding Rio tenderly in his arms and the next engaged in a fight—he turned his attention to Eliot, who was attempting to rise. But Cash didn't have time to fool with this guy. "Don't mess with me again, Eliot. Or Rio. It ends here, you got that?"

Not waiting for a response, he shot off in the direction Rio had taken.

Where had she gone?

Up ahead she was entering the equine complex, weaving her way through a milling crowd in front of the refreshment stands. Oblivious to the irritation of those around him, he pushed his way through, too. When he finally caught up with her, he grabbed her arm and drew her to a halt.

She pulled away, staring at him as if at a stranger. "Don't touch me."

He raised his hands warily as tears pooled in her ashen face.

"It's okay, Rio. Eliot's not going to follow us in here."

"Did you hit him again?"

"I didn't have to. He went down hard the first time, and I imagine he isn't too happy about it. But even drunk he won't bother us in this crowd."

"I want to go home."

"Okay." He nodded in the direction of the parking lot. "Truck's right outside."

Her expression clouded. "No. I'll find Grady and Sunshine and catch a ride with them."

"You don't want me to take you home?" Someone passing behind him jostled his shoulder. The sound of the speakers blaring was followed with a cheer from the crowd in the stands. "I'm sorry that Eliot—"

"It's not Eliot," she said through trembling lips. "It's…you and me, Cash. We're not a good idea."

No way had he imagined how she'd slipped willingly into his arms as if she belonged there. How she'd matched him one sweet kiss after another. "What am I missing here?"

She glanced almost fearfully around her.

"Eliot won't come into a crowd like this to finish his business. Too many who could bring him down." He tilted his head. "But then you said this wasn't about Eliot. That it's about us?"

"There is no *us*, Cash."

She ducked her head, her shoulders shaking. Oh, great, now she was crying. Risking her pulling away from him again, he put his hand on her lower back and steered her to a less congested edge of the crowd. She was trembling but, utterly helpless and knowing better than to try to pull her into his arms, he stood there awkwardly.

"You know I care for you, don't you, Rio? And I'm sorry Eliot interrupted before I could tell you that." Why wouldn't she look at him? "I didn't intend to let him drag me into a fight. I admit that at one time I did like a good fight. Not anymore. When God stepped into my life three years ago, all that changed. I changed."

She looked up at him then, her expression accusing. "I didn't see much evidence of that change tonight."

Her words gut-punched him harder than anything his fists had delivered to Eliot. "It won't happen again. I had the best of intentions to steer clear of him, but he's been pushing my buttons for weeks. I was caught off guard and lost my temper, reacted instinctively, and—"

"That's it, Cash, don't you see? It was instinctive. It's bred into you. You couldn't help yourself."

"I will from here on out. I'm not my father, Rio. I've told you that."

She shook her head. "I'm sorry, but I can't take that risk. Not again."

"Again?"

She blinked back tears as she looked him squarely in the eye. "Another man I cared for…in college…had a temper, too. Did you think I broke my nose falling off a horse?"

He stared down at her, his hands involuntarily clenching. "A man *hit* you?"

She nodded. "I can't risk getting sucked into that kind of relationship again. I was young, naive and so thrilled to have my first real boyfriend that I didn't recognize the signs of an abuser until it was too late."

A muscle in his jaw throbbed where Eliot had struck

him. "I'm no abuser, Rio. No matter what a jury believed, I've never struck a woman."

"He hadn't, either," she said, "or so he claimed. He'd sometimes push me too roughly when I didn't move fast enough to suit him, once knocking me to the ground. An accident, he said. Or he'd grip my arm so tightly it bruised. In both cases he quickly apologized. But he did have a temper and trouble always seemed to find him."

Like the way Eliot had dogged *him*?

"Unfortunately," she continued, "the one time I tried to step in, to break up one of those fights, he was so angry at my interference, so infuriated that he—"

She shuddered, squeezing her eyes shut.

His jaw hardened as the scene played out in his mind. Blood boiling, he saw himself stepping in, pulling the guy off the injured Rio and sending him crashing into a wall to beg for mercy he wouldn't receive.

His stomach knotted at the direction his thoughts had so quickly taken. Instinct. Bred into him. Wasn't that what she'd said? But wasn't that the nature of most men? To protect the woman they—*loved*?

He swallowed hard, then stepped back from Rio. She was right. Tonight there was little evidence that he'd changed since giving himself to God. And his behavior—his instinct that he hadn't taken control of—had brought Rio's fears to life again. Brought her to tears. No doubt she feared *him* now.

"Please let me drive you home."

"No. I'll ride with Grady and Sunshine."

Disappointed, he nodded, his throat parched, voice rough. "Can you forgive me? Maybe give me—"

"Another chance?" She shook her head, the hurt in her eyes matching that in his heart. "Yes, I can forgive you. There's no question of that. But it doesn't change our relationship."

"But—" But what? She'd witnessed him at his worst. The old version of himself he'd believed had been long buried, rising from the dead right before her eyes.

"Seth always said he was sorry, too. Said he wanted a second chance—and that last 'second' chance landed me in an emergency room. Despite his promises to seek help with anger management, I eventually heard he'd punched a new girlfriend when she tried to break up with him."

"Rio, I'd *never*—"

"There they are." With a pasted-on smile, she waved into the crowd, then without a backward glance hurried to an approaching Sunshine and Grady, their hands around hot dogs and sodas.

"Could I catch a ride home with you after the bull riding?" he heard her say. "Cash has to leave early."

And then she was gone, disappearing into the crowd with her brother and sister-in-law.

Shame settled heavily as he stared blindly after her. This was his fault, and he had no one else to blame. Not even Eliot.

He'd blown it. Had deceived himself.

He wasn't fit to love a woman like Rio…or to be a father to Joey.

She'd done it again.

She'd allowed herself to fall for a hot-tempered man with a violent streak. Even days later, she remembered too vividly the fury that transformed Cash's usually easygoing demeanor, his dark eyes smoldering with rage. The same eyes that only moments before had looked down at her with gentle playfulness—with love? How could she reconcile the two extremes of this man?

"I wish Dad could have come today." Joey looked at her glumly from where he sat astride Misty as he walked the mare around the perimeter of the corral. Helmeted head up, back erect, legs positioned correctly, his nonrein hand relaxed on his thigh, not clutching the saddle horn. He'd come so far in such a short time once they'd gotten to the heart of his aversion to horses.

"Maybe he can come next time. I know he's proud of you. We both are."

The boy grinned at her praise as he nudged his pony into a trot, and her heart swelled with an almost maternal joy. Despite a determination not to get attached to Joey, she'd too often found herself daydreaming of what it would be like to be his mom. To tuck him in at night and tickle him awake. To shower him with hugs. Of course, in order for *that* to happen, Cash would have to be her husband. Although she cared for the boy's father, that could never be.

As it was, Cash had been avoiding her. And she, him.

This was the third riding lesson that week that he'd missed. Another opportunity to bond with his son slipping through his fingers. He said he was busy. That she was better with Joey on this lesson stuff than he was anyway.

Had she overreacted that night in pushing him away?

No, her instincts were on target. As much as it hurt to break off the beginnings of a relationship with him, it was the right thing to do. Before it had gone too far. Before either had shared words of love or made commitments.

Strangely enough, she didn't doubt that Cash cared for her. Not only had he said he did, but she'd seen it in his eyes in those unguarded moments when he'd kissed her. Which made it all the harder to push him away. But she'd gone down that road before. Men with anger issues didn't make good life partners, and she refused to be a textbook victim ever again.

She'd be advising other young women in the future and didn't dare risk becoming a two-time casualty of sticking her head in the sand. She couldn't be a blind-leading-the-blind counselor.

"There he is!" Joey reined in on the other side of the corral as Cash approached the fence.

Not the usual confident stride she'd become accustomed to. Something had changed. In recent days his body language had become more withdrawn, demeanor less animated, his interactions with others—even his son—more reserved.

Had she done that to him?

"Hey, champ, lookin' good."

"I've been trotting. Did you see me?"

"I did. You said you loped last time, too."

"I can show you."

Cash looked to her, his eyes questioning as if asking permission to say yes to his son.

She nodded. "Show him, Joey."

Brows lowering in concentration, the boy settled himself into the saddle, firmed his footing in the stirrups and adjusted the reins. Then with a kick of his heels he signaled to the pony, and Misty broke into a gentle lope. Or at least as gentle as a pony could manage, with Joey occasionally maintaining his balance with a brief touch to the saddle horn.

"See, Dad?"

"I see. You're becoming quite the horseman."

"Like you!"

She didn't miss the shadow that touched Cash's eyes as he rounded the outside of the fence and let himself into the corral to join her.

"He's doing great, Cash."

"He is, thanks to you."

Joey and his pony made three turns around the corral, slowed to a jarring trot, then back to a walk before he reined in next to them and leaned over to pat Misty's neck.

"Eliot thinks I'm ready for something bigger."

Cash's brows lowered ominously. "He does, does he?"

"He says babies ride ponies. I'm eight."

"Let's master the basics on the pony first," Rio said quickly. She'd graduated to a small horse herself when not much older than Joey but, of course, with much more experience under her belt. "Then we'll see about practicing on one of the horses."

"Woo-hoo!" He fist pumped the air.

"I don't want him going too far too fast," Cash said under his breath as Joey dismounted and led the pony toward the barn.

"He'll be well supervised."

"I know. I didn't mean—never mind."

"Is something wrong?"

"I'm just—" He shrugged. "I'm still trying to locate his mom. Thought I had a lead, then it petered out."

"You're still concerned she'll take him away, aren't you?"

"Not so much now." He stared in the direction of the barn. "Maybe that would actually be for the best."

She couldn't believe her ears. "How could that be for the best?"

"I don't have time for a kid, Rio." He bumped up the

brim of his hat with his wrist. "I don't know anything about raising one. I was fooling myself."

"Do you seriously think Lorilee was doing a better job than you are?"

"He needs a woman's influence. And while you've been great with him and he really likes you, he needs his mom."

Guilt pierced. This was her fault. Cash was taking her fears regarding him to heart. Yes, he had anger issues that concerned her, but never once had she seen those directed toward Joey. Clearly, though, he was building a protective wall, putting distance between himself and a future he'd dreamed of with his child. Because of *her* accusations, he was doubting he could be the kind of father he'd hoped to be. Was convincing himself Joey would be better off without him so that if the time came…

"Don't think like that, Cash. Joey is far better off with you."

"Think so? A kid who won't let me hug him? Who can't even bring himself to parrot back an 'I love you'?"

"I know it's hard, but don't get discouraged. You're doing a fabulous job. It's coming. I sense he wants to please you. But honestly, his mother doesn't sound like much of a mother to me."

"She not a *bad* woman." Cash placed his hands on his hips, his gaze dropping to the ground as if pondering his own words. "She means well. Good intentions."

Cheating on her first husband and abandoning her son demonstrated good intentions? He didn't consider that bad? "Sometimes good intentions don't hack it."

Cash's eyes narrowed. "No, they don't."

She winced. To him it probably sounded as though she was harkening back to their earlier conversation regarding his inability to control his anger. "I'm sorry, I didn't mean—"

"I know you didn't. But the fact of the matter is a boy needs a mom."

And *she'd* once foolishly dreamed she might fill that role. "But first and foremost, Cash, he needs his dad."

How could he not see that?

"Either way, I've got to find her. I mean, what would happen if—God forbid—something happened to me? What would happen to *him*?"

"Nothing's going to happen to you. And if it did, Joey's in good hands with this family. He's not going to be cast out on the street homeless while authorities are looking for his mother."

He removed his hat and wearily ran his hand through his hair. "I'm thinking crazy, aren't I?"

"You are."

But if he wanted to talk crazy to her all day long, that was fine with her. Although the direction their relationship had been headed had halted abruptly, it was a relief to talk to him again.

"Joey missed you at his lessons this week."

"Yeah, well, I thought it was for the best. You know, considering the circumstances."

"Circumstances. Meaning us."

"There's no *us*, remember?" He scuffed a toe in the dirt. "I don't want to make you uncomfortable, Rio. I feel bad enough about forcing you to relive the past because of what happened with Eliot and me."

"I told Grandma Jo and Mom and Dad," she said quietly. "He's been warned, and they'll be watching him closely."

A mocking smile lifted the corners of his mouth. "And me, as well?"

"I made it clear that he hit you first." She studied the yellowing bruise on the side of his face. "How's your jaw?"

He motioned her away, obviously not willing to say a whole lot about it. "He packs a wallop."

She frowned. "He hasn't approached you again, has he?"

"Not yet. I told him that night before I went searching for you to consider it settled. Not to mess with me again."

"And if he does?"

Cash slowly shook his head. "I don't know, Rio. I don't want to make promises I'm not sure I can keep."

Which was exactly why they were where they were right now. He recognized he was incapable of keeping that kind of promise, and she couldn't let herself be drawn into the uncertainty.

They were back to square one.

Cash again set his hat on his head. Adjusted it a fraction to that rakish tilt both Joey and the male summer help emulated. Had he noticed they did that? Not likely. He probably wasn't even aware he didn't set his own hat square on his head.

He glanced at the barn. "Guess I'll help Joey finish up with the pony, then we'll grab lunch together and I'll drop him off with Anna."

"And you'll come to his next lesson?"

"I'll think about it."

"Don't think too long. You yourself admitted these summer months are critical to your relationship."

But had he already given up on that?

Cash gave a brisk nod before moving away. Her insides aching for the man and boy, she watched as he disappeared inside the barn. Then she drew a ragged breath as an unwelcome truth dawned.

I love Cash Herrera.

Not a passing infatuation such as she'd had with Seth and had mistaken for something more. No, this was where you wanted the best for the other person. Where the relationship wasn't all about you. And yet…she had to look out for herself, too. It would be so simple to look the other way, refuse to read the writing on the wall that experience clearly warned of.

Thunder rumbled in the distance, and she caught the faint scent of rain as she lifted her face to the steel-gray monsoon clouds building overhead.

I love him, Lord. I can admit that now. But why did he have to come into my life when You won't let me have him?

Chapter Fourteen

"So you're enjoying your riding lessons, Joey?"

On Sunday after church, Cash had declined an invitation to join the Hunters for lunch, even though he'd seen Rio heading out with Deputy Braxton Turner after services. Now he smiled at his son, who was seated across from him at one of the inn's small dining tables. He sure loved that boy.

One eye squinted, Joey dipped a french fry in a pool of ketchup and pointed it at his father.

"Rio makes lessons fun. And I'm getting good at it, too." He grinned as he popped the fried morsel into his mouth.

Cash chuckled. Smug whippersnapper. "Yes, you are."

But Cash still hadn't participated in his riding lessons, stopping by at the conclusion of each to pick him up for lunch and drop him back off with his sitter. Although Rio didn't seem to have a problem with him joining them, it felt uncomfortable to be around a woman who for a few breathtaking moments had so eagerly responded to his kisses. Cuddled into his arms. Her enthusiasm had driven his senses reeling with grateful prayers of amazement and possibilities for the future.

Then she'd sent him packing.

It didn't help matters, either, when the good deputy—who Cash had long suspected had his eye on Rio—dropped by more than once. On the pretext, of course, of checking on the progress of his mare. Then he *just happened* to mosey around until he cornered her for a friendly chat. It looked like his efforts had paid off if her climbing into his pickup in the church's parking lot was any indication.

The situation at the Hideaway was increasingly awkward, though. Not only being around Rio, but around her family, too. He was ashamed that, along with enlightening them as to Eliot's misbehavior, she'd had to tell of the role he'd played, as well. Right from the beginning the Hunters had been welcoming, accepting of him despite his background and jail time. Although no one had spoken to him regarding the incident in Canyon Springs—which as his employer they had every right to do—he'd let them down. Broken their trust. Just as he'd shattered Rio's trust into a thousand irreparable pieces.

She'd be leaving for school in a few weeks…should he do the Hunter family a favor and hit the road, too?

"Dad, do you think I'm ready to ride a big horse yet?"

He smiled at his son across the table. "Rio thinks you have a ways to go, so I'm deferring to her judgment."

"What's defer?"

"Going along with. Agreeing to."

Making a face, Joey propped one elbow on the table and set his chin on the heel of his hand, then swirled another fry through ketchup. "Bummer."

Outside the window next to them, monsoon rains

had earlier lashed almost horizontally, pummeling the swaying ponderosa pines. They'd barely gotten to the restaurant before the storm hit, but it was tapering off now. Inside, though, they were warm and dry, the mellow glow of lamplight lending the raftered space a snug feeling. He was truly blessed to be sitting here with Joey, downing burgers and fries.

But for how long?

The last time he'd had more than a few passing words with Rio, she'd insisted Joey was better off with him than his ex-wife. While he appreciated hearing that, he had his doubts. He'd been giving it considerable thought and prayer since that night when, in a blind fury, he'd lit into Eliot. Had unthinkingly returned fist fire without the slightest inner check to slow him down.

He rubbed a still-tender jaw. That wasn't a good thing for a man to know about himself.

He couldn't fault Rio for slamming the door in his face. Not after what had happened to her but a few years ago. Although she recognized that he hadn't instigated the altercation, that Eliot was responsible, she no doubt wondered, as did he, if he'd really changed since he'd turned his life over to God. Deep inside, where it counted.

Didn't much look like it.

Which was why, although he hated the thought of returning Joey to Lorilee—to a stepdad who didn't want him—his search for her now held a slightly different edge to it.

"You done there, Joey?" He wasn't in a hurry to leave, but the inn's lobby was filling with hungry folks waiting for a table.

As soon as Joey did justice to that last fry, Cash helped him on with his jacket, then snagged his own hat off the wall peg inside the dining room door and ushered Joey through the packed lobby and onto the front porch.

As they stood outside watching the rain now reduced to a sun-splashed drizzle, Joey looked up at him. "I'm glad I live with you now, Dad."

Cash's heart twisted. Had the kid picked up on his father's indecisiveness as to what the future held for them?

"I'm glad you're here with me, too." His boy meant the world to him. "I love you, son."

"I..." The boy stopped, then started again. "I...love you, too, Dad."

Stunned, Cash stared into the youngster's hope-filled eyes. Then abruptly Joey grabbed him in a bear hug, leaving Cash further shaken. He closed his eyes, his heart crying out his thanks to God as he held his son close, drinking in his rough-and-tumble little boy scent. Treasuring this most precious of unexpected gifts.

Rio had predicted it, but he hadn't seen this coming.

"I'll be real good. I'll make you proud of me." Joey squeezed him more tightly. "I promise."

Despite his son's confirmation that living with Dad wasn't a bad thing, Cash recoiled inwardly as he looked down at the boy's upturned face. The desperation now surfacing in Joey's expression pierced him.

Placing his hand reassuringly on the child's shoulder, he looked Joey in the eye. "Son, you're already a good boy, and I'm already proud of you. Your being good or bad or making me more proud has nothing to do with your not having been able to live with me before. It's not your fault. You need to understand that. I've always loved you, and I always will."

The truth was that if Cash had been a better man all along, Joey's mother wouldn't have been able to pull the stunts she had with the blessings of the legal system. Not long ago he'd read in the Bible about the sins of the fathers being visited on the children. The turn of events in his son's young life was a prime example of that, with Joey paying the price no little boy should have to pay.

Just like Cash had done—reaping the consequences of a father's poor choices.

How could he have considered handing his beloved son back to Lorilee? What kind of father was he, anyway?

He blinked back the moisture forming in his eyes. "Looks like the rain is letting up. As soon as the last of those clouds roll through, the sun will dry things out fast. What do you say we go for a ride?"

Joey's face brightened. "Together? You and me?"

"If you want to."

"Oh, wow, yeah."

He gave his father another hug that a still-overcome Cash warmly reciprocated.

Two-and-a-half hours later, they returned from their ride, the two of them—father and son—grooming Blue and Misty before turning them loose in the pasture.

"I'm going to put our tack away, so stick close while I do that. Then we'll head back to the cabin, get cleaned up and dig that carton of chocolate ice cream out of the freezer."

"Yay!"

Cash's heart hummed as he hauled their gear to the tack room. Carefully hung the bridles and Joey's riding helmet. Had there ever been a day in his life better than this one?

When he'd finished up, he stepped into the wide aisle between the stalls. "Let's go, Joey."

No response. Now where had he gotten off to? He headed down the aisle toward the rear of the barn, then halted and raised his voice. "Let's go! That ice cream is calling our names."

"Look at me, Dad!"

Cash spun, his heart lodging in his throat at the sight that met his eyes.

Joey.

Through the open bars of the last box stall, he could see into the adjoining paddock where Joey sat, proud as punch, on the bare back of a nervously shifting horse, his fingers entwined in her mane.

Wild Card. Deputy Turner's mare.

Forcing himself not to panic, not to startle either boy or horse, Cash's heart pounded against his rib cage. No time for reprimands. No time for reminders that Joey had been told to keep away from that horse.

We've got to get him off her, Lord.

"How'd you get up there, buddy?" Keeping his voice even, Cash let himself into the box stall and closed the door quietly behind him, his eyes never leaving the horse and boy in the adjoining fenced area.

"I climbed on the fence and got her to come close," he announced with a satisfied lift to his chin. "I think she likes me. I give her apples."

When had Joey managed to get that by him? Giving treats was something Cash didn't indulge in with a horse prone to nipping.

"How'd you plan to get down from there?"

Joey's forehead creased, then he shrugged, unconcerned. "Jump on the fence again?"

"Well, we need to get you down from there a different way." Without spooking the horse. "So you need to do what I tell you to do, okay?"

Joey nodded, but didn't appear alarmed.

Overconfident kid. Too much like his daddy had been at that age.

The heavy-duty plastic feed bucket in the stall was mostly licked clean, but Cash unhooked it, threw a couple of fistfuls of hay inside, then took measured steps to the open stall doorway. He halted when Wild Card jerked her head up, her ears flicking back and forth as she kept uneasy tabs on both the man in front of her and the boy on her back.

"Easy girl." He slowly stepped into the paddock and moved away from the door, knowing she could get it into her head to plow over the top of him to get back inside.

"If she heads for the stall, hang on tight, duck down on her neck and stay down. Okay?" He wasn't certain he could grab his boy off a speeding horse without risking injury.

"'Kay."

Now if he could get close enough… She wasn't wearing a halter so he had nothing to grab. Didn't have rope or the time to get one.

Before he could move forward again, the mare tossed her head and abruptly backed until her bottom slammed against the wooden fence, the jolt almost unseating Joey whose eyes suddenly widened.

"Help, Dad," he squeaked as he scrambled to right himself, his gaze darting to his father as he clung more tightly to the horse's mane.

"Hang on there, champ. We'll get you off in a minute."

Please, God.

Wild Card had more tricks up her sleeve than any

horse he'd ever worked with. But he *had* been working with her, beginning to build a trust. Or so he hoped.

He shook the bucket, the sound catching her attention. Ears flicking, she lowered her head slightly, blowing hard.

"Come on over here, you troublemaker you." He rattled the bucket again, set it on the ground to free his hands. Took a step back. "When she gets close enough to check this out, I want you to let go of her mane and I'll grab you off, all right? Then hold on to my neck tight."

As the horse took a few tentative steps forward, Joey's voice took on an excited edge. "She wants some, Dad."

"That's the plan." He breathed easier with each hesitant step.

Then, without warning, the mare swung around, lowered her head and kicked back at Cash with both hind feet, throwing Joey into the fence. Cash barely leaped out of the way of flying hooves before the wild-eyed animal spun and bolted past him and back into the box stall.

Instinctively, Cash slid the door shut, penning her in. Then, barely able to breathe, he stumbled to where Joey lay motionless on the still-muddy ground, his body resting at unnatural angles and blood trickling from a cut on his head.

Please, God, no.

"Thank you, Brax, for an enjoyable meal." Rio placed her napkin on their table at Kit's Lodge and Restaurant, wondering why she'd agreed to come. Maybe because he was a regular, down-to-earth guy. Not edgy like Seth and Cash.

"You're welcome, Rio. I've been hoping we could go out sometime. Get to know each other better."

Despite the fact that on their drive to Canyon Springs her thoughts too often drifted to her last visit to the neighboring community, her time with Brax had been pleasant enough.

It wasn't his fault that when they drove by the pet shop she could hear Cash's laugh. Or that when they passed stores on Main Street she could almost feel Cash's hand in hers. With renewed determination, though, she'd shoved aside those too-vivid memories when they reached Kit's. For the most part, she and Brax had fallen into a nice enough, if stilted, conversation that waxed and waned. Typical first date stuff when two people were searching for areas of common interest.

But she'd been especially hard-pressed to hear a word he said once she glimpsed the name tag of their waitress.

Lorilee.

Probably more women than she could count had that same distinctive name, but the coincidence unnerved her. Especially when—could she be imagining it?—the woman's dimpled smile reminded her of Cash's Joey.

"Nice waitress," Brax commented as he slipped a generous tip underneath the corner of his plate.

"Very nice." And not at all how she imagined Cash's ex-wife. Friendly. Talkative. No horns or pitchfork. She went a little heavy on the eye makeup and was a bit too flirty—which would have irritated Rio had she taken an interest in Brax. But with shoulder-length hair fashionably cut and glossy nails appearing professionally done, she was beyond cute—as would be expected of someone who'd caught the eye of a teenage Cash.

But on the surface, the auburn-haired woman with

a tattoo of a ladybug on her wrist didn't seem like the kind of person who'd kick a child out of her life once it became inconvenient. When a new love life beckoned.

So maybe it wasn't her. The matching smile thing was probably a fluke. But she'd talk to Cash as soon as she got back to the Hideaway to make sure.

The return trip to Hunter Ridge took longer than it should have, with Brax stopping for gasoline, taking a detour to show her where his grandmother used to live, and a side trip to see an historical marker. In the midst of all that, they'd barely gotten on the highway when they'd had to pull over for an ambulance going in the opposite direction, no doubt headed to the regional hospital at Show Low.

"I hope that wasn't Delaney headed off to deliver Junior."

Brax grinned. "That's right. The poor thing looks like she's ready to pop."

Rio was more than happy to get back to town— although later in the afternoon than planned. This was a daytime date, though, so surely there would be no expectation of a so-called good-night kiss, would there? As stupid as it might seem, she wasn't in a hurry to have her Cash-kissed lips touched by another man's.

"So how about it, Rio?" Brax pulled his truck up beside hers where they'd left it in the church parking lot. He shut off the engine and turned to her. "Are you up for dinner this week? I had a great time today and would enjoy seeing you again. That is, you know, if you'd want to."

"I had a nice time, too. But you know…" She hated this. Absolutely hated it. "I'm going to be leaving town in a few weeks to go back to college. This isn't a good time to be starting anything. My future isn't in Hunter

Ridge, and getting involved now wouldn't be fair to either of us."

There, that wasn't too bad of a letdown. It allowed them both to exit gracefully. Required no further explanation.

He shifted in his seat. "I knew you were headed back to school when I invited you to lunch today. But you know, Flag's a hop, skip and jump for a guy who racks up county miles the way I do on a daily basis."

She tensed, but managed a smile. "Which is one more reason you need to relax during your time off and not pile the miles on your personal vehicle."

"You'll be coming home weekends, though, won't you?"

"Doubtful." Why couldn't he let this drop? "I'll be carrying quite a few hours, so lots of studying. I'll also be working with local churches on the side to provide preventative education as well as counseling for victims of dating violence. There's more of that going on than most people imagine."

"Yeah, I see more domestic violence in my line of work than I'd like to." He pinned her with his gaze. "Heard about your talk to the youth group. I'm sorry that happened to you."

"It's in the past now." She reached for the door handle. "Thank you for taking me to lunch, Brax."

"You're welcome." He gave a somewhat resigned chuckle. "But we won't be doing it again."

"My schedule, you know."

"And that Herrera dude, if I'm not mistaken."

Her breath caught. "What's he have to do with it?"

"Seems every time I stop by the Hideaway, looking for you, I only have to find him and know you won't be too far away."

"Cash and I aren't—"

"He did jail time, Rio. Did you know that? For hitting his ex-wife."

So word had gotten around the law enforcement grapevine.

"He didn't hit her, Brax. She lied."

"He told you that?"

"I believe him." And she did. "Ask that deputy who is a friend of Cash's—Will Lamar? He believes him, too."

"I know Will's got good instincts, but it's not easy to pull the wool over a judge and jury's eyes. They look at things from all angles. Weigh the evidence, the conflicting testimonies. Ferret out the truth."

"But they're human, too. They can make mistakes like the rest of us."

"Be careful, Rio. I don't want to see you get hurt."

"No fear of that. Like I told you, I'm heading back to school in a few weeks. Cash and I are…friends. Nothing more."

"He looks at you like there's more."

She swung the door open and jumped out. "Well, there's not."

Thanks to her.

He leaned over, his expression concerned. "I didn't mean to make you mad, Rio. I—"

"You didn't. I know you're looking out for me. But you're mistaken. About a lot of things. Bye, Brax."

She forced a smile as she slammed the door shut, then turned to her own vehicle and climbed inside. As soon as she'd started the engine, the deputy pulled away.

Way to go, Rio.

The guy was trying to help, show he cared, and she'd gotten defensive and bent out of shape when Cash's name came up. If Braxton was fishing to confirm his suspicions regarding her feelings for the other man, that likely clinched it.

But it was too late for Cash and her.

Back at the Hideaway, she pulled into the main parking lot, noting several family members were standing outside the inn talking. Sober eyed. Not laughing and joking—or heatedly debating—as usually befit an informal gathering of Hunters.

With a ripple of uneasiness, she hopped out of the truck and covered the distance between them. "What's going on?"

Sunshine's expression was grim. "Joey had an accident."

An icy cold shot through her. "What happened?"

"That horse of Brax's," Grady clarified, "threw him."

"What was he doing on Wild Card?"

How many times had she reminded Cash that kids needed to be supervised? That they were sneaky and fast and always where you didn't think they could possibly be.

"We don't know details, Rio." Her mother spoke with a reassuring calmness that her daughter didn't share. "We didn't know anything had happened until the ambulance raced in here, siren going and lights flashing."

An ambulance. The one they'd had to pull over for a good twenty or thirty minutes ago?

"How badly is he hurt? Is he going to be okay?"

"We don't know, honey." Dad pinned her with one of his just-calm-down-now looks. "He was unconscious. Cash said he'll call from the hospital when he knows something."

Unconscious.

She stared at her dad—at all of them. "And you let Cash go alone?"

She spun away and raced back to her truck before anyone could stop her. She backed the vehicle out, put it in Drive, then paused to roll down the window.

"I know you're already doing it, but pray. Please pray."

Chapter Fifteen

His heart still galloping, Cash paced the floor of the emergency room's stark waiting area, pungent hospital odors strong in his nostrils.

What was taking so long?

Around him, under the harsh, fluorescent lights, others waited in anxious, worn-out silence for their turn to be admitted or to receive news of someone who already had been. A toddler screeched, getting on his nerves.

For what seemed like the millionth time, he took a deep breath, willing himself to relax. He'd been praying nonstop for the past hour. Not only for Joey, but to banish the horrifying image of his son's seemingly lifeless body lying on the ground.

It had happened so fast.

How had Joey gotten away from him? Managed to get up on that temperamental mare so quickly?

Rio had warned him of the need for supervision, but with the amazing strides Joey was making around horses, he'd allowed himself to become careless. Inattentive, even if only for a few minutes. Joey's continued interest in wanting to ride a "big horse" should have put him on guard.

"Excuse me, mister, but would you please sit down?" A woman who appeared as stressed as he felt looked up at him from one of the seating clusters. "You're wearing a hole in the linoleum and making the rest of us as jumpy as you are."

"Sorry." He offered an apologetic smile and moved closer to the entrance doors, out of the immediate seating area. No way could he sit sardined in with the others. Not with the way his conscience was slamming him from one mental wall to the next.

He should have sent Wild Card back to Braxton after the first week. But no, he wouldn't admit defeat that early in the game. Not only did he like a challenge, but he had it in his head he could boost his reputation as a successful handler of difficult horses if he could turn the mare around.

Now Joey was paying the price for his father's ambition.

His stupidity.

What *was* taking so long? When they'd arrived, they wouldn't let him go in with Joey. Said he'd be in the way. So shouldn't someone show a little mercy and come out to talk to him?

And then he saw her.

An anxious-looking Rio, still dressed for church, trotted toward the ER's entrance. Relief cascaded through him, the sense of aloneness and disorientation he'd felt since entering the medical facility dissipating.

She spied him immediately and headed straight to him. For a moment he thought she was going to launch herself into his arms, but then she caught herself and halted in front of him.

"I just found out. I'm so sorry, Cash. Is Joey going to be okay?"

"I don't know yet." Frowning, he glanced back at the sliding doors leading into the inner recesses of the ER. "I assume someone will be out soon to tell me what's going on."

"What happened? Grady said he was thrown off Wild Card?"

He may as well face the music. No way could he wiggle out of the responsibility of this one. "Like you warned, Joey got away from me. He was right there one minute and gone the next."

"Oh, Cash."

"He managed to scale the fence to the enclosure outside Wild Card's stall. Lured her over and climbed aboard. Did you know he's been feeding her apples on the sly?"

"No, of course I didn't. I'd have stopped him."

"Anyway—" He took a ragged breath, thankful he had someone to talk to now. Someone who would listen. Who cared. "The mare got overexcited, and the next thing I knew she'd thrown Joey into the fence. Knocked him out. From the way he was all twisted around, I think he may have broken bones. Likely worse. He wasn't wearing a helmet."

She looked up at him with compassion-filled eyes. "I'm so sorry."

"Me, too. But it's my fault."

"How can you say that?"

He kneaded the muscles at the back of his neck. "Because at lunch he was bummed when I told him he wasn't ready for a full-size horse. Eliot told him babies ride ponies, remember? A *good* father would have had his antennae up, recognized what might be going on in a little kid's head and been more vigilant."

"But as I told you before, Cash, kids are fast. We

can't keep our eye on them every single second, no matter how hard we try."

"Well, I blew this one. Big-time."

"Don't be so hard on yourself."

He closed his eyes briefly, then focused again on Rio, as if somehow connecting with her was connecting with his son.

"At least the emergency team from Hunter Ridge allowed me to ride in the ambulance." He glanced toward the waiting area and admissions desk, then lowered his voice. "But when we got here I had a tussle with admissions. My worst nightmare."

"Obviously they admitted him."

"I told them I didn't have the proof of insurance with me, that I hadn't been expecting an emergency. No way, though, was I telling them I don't have custody. I signed every single paper they shoved at me as if I had every legal right to. They can sue me later for misrepresentation for all I care."

A shadow flickered through Rio's eyes. "He's insured, though, right?"

"Yeah, his insurance is in his mother's name. I pay the premiums. But I could kick myself. Why wasn't I more persistent in pursuing Lorilee so these legalities would have been taken care of—or at least in process by now? But no, I didn't listen to my friend Will. I dragged my feet, unwilling to rock the boat and risk prematurely losing Joey."

Rio looked up at him with troubled eyes, then something sparked within their depths. She gripped his arm. "What color is Lorilee's hair?"

He stared, foggy headed, not understanding her question.

"Her hair color," she persisted. "What is it?"

His lips compressed, suppressing irritation. His son might be fighting for his life and Rio wanted to know what color the boy's mother's hair was?

"Tell me, Cash. It's important."

He gave a disbelieving scoff. "Dark red. That's the natural color, anyway. Who knows what it is now. Satisfied?"

Rio's eyes widened, her fingers biting into his arm. "And does she have a tattoo? A ladybug on her wrist?"

Goose bumps raised on his arms.

"She does," he said slowly. "The horse she owned when we were first married was named Ladybug."

With a whimper, Rio pressed her hand to her mouth. "Cash, we've found her. I know where she is."

"You know where she is and you didn't tell me?" Cash's voice had raised slightly, unexpectedly sharp, condemning.

"No. I mean, yes. I—"

"Where is she?"

"Canyon Springs. She's waitressing at Kit's Lodge."

"Kit's? Are you telling me she's been in my own backyard this whole time?" Then confusion dawned in his eyes. "Why were you keeping it a secret?"

"I didn't. I wasn't. She waited on our table today. Brax and I—" She halted, reluctant to divulge that she and the deputy had been on a date.

"When were you planning to tell me?"

She stared at him. "Excuse me? I just got here and thought Joey's condition took priority. Besides, I had no idea what she looked like. I needed to confirm that with you."

"Then what made you think she was my ex-wife?"

"The name. It's unique. And—" She hesitated. Some

exes didn't care to see resemblances to the other partner in their offspring. "She has Joey's smile. The dimple."

Cash's own smile was grim. "So it is her."

"I'm sure of it now. And you know what that means, don't you? She can cosign the hospital paperwork. Confirm the insurance."

Processing all she'd shared with him, he slowly nodded as he pulled up the number for Kit's Lodge on his cell phone. In a matter of minutes, his ex-wife was called to the restaurant's phone and he filled her in on the situation as briefly as possible.

He listened intently, then frowned. "When's your shift over? I'll come get you."

But he'd no more than hung up when he glanced at the ER's inner doors and groaned. "What was I thinking? Her husband's out of town and he has the car. But I can't leave to go get her now. They might—"

"I'll go."

"You'd do that?"

"Of course." Why did he sound surprised that she'd be willing to help him? "I'm going. Right now. Call me if you hear anything on Joey, okay?"

"I will." To her surprise, he took her hand in his. Gave it a squeeze. But his expression remained bleak. "Thanks, Rio."

Her heart went out to him. "Don't beat yourself up, Cash."

"Hard not to."

"This wasn't your fault." Impulsively, she wrapped her arms around him, pinning his to his sides. A deliberately unromantic hug. She didn't want any misunderstanding, although on which of their parts she had concerns she wasn't quite sure.

When she released him, he smiled. "I needed that."

"Good. I'll be back." She headed to the automated doors, then paused to look at him. "Joey's going to be okay."

Please God, let me be right. Anything less will kill Cash.

The drive to Canyon Springs battered her with thoughts of Joey. Cash. Lorilee. It hadn't escaped her that Cash had immediately assumed she'd withheld information regarding his ex-wife. That stung. But she'd led him to believe she couldn't trust him, so wasn't it natural he'd also believe she still thought he'd struck Lorilee—was protecting the woman from him by withholding her whereabouts?

She groaned at that realization as she hurried inside Kit's to identify herself to Cash's former wife, a call coming in from him to provide a long-awaited update just as she crossed the threshold. Joey had briefly regained consciousness, but was now sleeping. A broken arm and collarbone. Cuts requiring stitches. A scan showed possible inner cranial swelling, so they wanted to keep him in the intensive care unit to monitor that condition.

Outside Kit's, Lorilee climbed into Rio's truck and fastened her seat belt. She sighed. "That boy of mine..."

"Is a sweetheart."

"I was going to say he's too much like his daddy. Can wear out your patience in the blink of an eye." She rode in silence until they hit the highway when thoughts of Joey apparently moved to the back burner and she cut a speculative look at Rio. "Are you seeing that nice deputy you were with today? He comes in a couple of times a week. Alone."

"Actually—"

"Or are you sweet on that rascal Cash? He's a

charmer, isn't he? Always had a weakness for barrel racers."

Rio's breath caught, not liking the direction this conversation was taking. "How'd you know I was a barrel racer?"

Lorilee pointed to the distinctive sticker in the back window. "What's your connection to Cashton?"

"He's employed at my family's business in Hunter Ridge."

"That's all?"

Rio's face warmed, and she could only hope her cheeks weren't as rosy as she suspected they were. "That's all."

With an amused look, Lorilee folded her arms, but apparently decided to let it go, once again changing the subject. "He said my boy's going to be okay."

"But the hospital is going to err on the side of caution. Head injuries can be tricky."

"Nothing's ever simple, is it?" Lorilee stared out the side window. "What in the blazes was that man thinking letting my boy get on a horse? I expected him to keep Joey safe."

Rio's hands tightened on the steering wheel. "He's safe with his father, I can assure you of that. No matter how cautious a parent is, these things happen. Kids don't always do what they're told to do."

"Don't I know it." She shook her head. "Joey's gotten to be a real handful. Samuel wasn't willing to take him on for that very reason—among others."

"Samuel's your husband?"

She nodded. "We're newlyweds. He's a good man. Lots better than that last one I got myself tangled up with." She shook her head again. "But if I'd have known from the beginning how much work it takes to keep a man happy, maybe I'd have stuck with Cash. Invested my efforts in him up front and saved myself a lot of grief later."

Rio focused on the road ahead, Lorilee's words echoing in her mind. That *was* God's original plan. That what He'd joined together, shouldn't be torn apart. How much heartbreak people would spare themselves and their children if they went into relationships with eyes wide open, recognizing that love wasn't merely a feeling. It was a way of life that, by design, required time and effort. Putting someone else's welfare before your own.

Giving your partner the benefit of the doubt.

Had things worked out between her and Cash, would she have been capable of loving him like that? She'd been giving it considerable thought. Prayer. Increasingly, the differences between Cash and Seth were becoming clear. Seth was only capable of loving Seth. As far as he was concerned, everyone else on the planet had been put here to keep him happy. And when they didn't…

No, Cash was nothing like her former boyfriend. She was coming to understand that—and that she had no reason to fear that he ever would be.

But *was* it too late for them?

"Thanks for coming, Lorilee. For signing the papers." She'd not only signed them, but had earlier joined Cash in visiting Joey in ICU. Their boy had been sound asleep, looking so tiny and helpless in the hospital bed with the tubes, wires and monitors rigged up around him.

She frowned. "You sound like you didn't think I would."

One. Two. Three.

"Why would I?" He didn't want to argue. There had been too many arguments through the years, but she needed to know how her disappearing act had impacted him. Joey. "You dumped Joey on me out of the blue and cut ties without leaving a working phone number in case of an emergency. A number where your abandoned son could call you. I had no idea where you were. Rio knew I was trying to locate you and just happened to see you at the restaurant today. Recognized your name and thought Joey resembled you."

What were the odds of that? He glanced in Rio's direction where across the waiting room she chatted with an elderly man. Maybe Rio didn't "just happen" to do anything of the sort. A higher power was in play.

Lorilee's eyes flashed as she plopped her hands on her hips. "How could you not know where I was? I told Mama. She has my new number."

"Yeah, and Mama never liked me. But that's of no account now. You're here, vouching for Joey's medical coverage. That's all that matters. Thank you."

Appeased, she jerked her head in Rio's direction, lowering her voice. "That gal with the funny name... Rio? She wouldn't 'fess up, but is she your lady now?"

"We're friends. I work for—"

"Her family. She said that, too." Lorilee smirked. "You two sure have your stories down pat."

"Sticking to the truth is always the best policy."

"You're not planning to live out the rest of your life as a cranky old bachelor, are you? She seems to care for Joey. You could do worse, Cash."

He wasn't going to discuss his love life with his ex-wife. "That's something we need to talk about. *Joey's* future."

"I love that boy and because I do, I know his future is with you. Not me."

He looked at her doubtfully. "Even after what happened to him on my watch?"

"As your lady *friend* pointed out on the way over here, accidents happen. Kids are unpredictable, and you can't keep them locked up in a cage."

Relief flooded through him. "Then I'll be in touch soon. With my lawyer."

"I won't fight you on it. My new husband's considerably older than I am. Real steady type. But he's raised one family and doesn't want to take on another. And for myself, I've carried the load these first eight years of Joey's life."

Interesting spin she had there.

"You can see him on down the road to eighteen with my blessing, Cash, as long as I get to see him once in a while."

"Thank you, Lorilee."

Thank You, God.

"You're welcome, Cash." She studied him a long moment. "I owe you anyway."

"How do you figure?"

"You've put up with a lot from me. When we married, I was caught up with myself and what I wanted. Expected you to make me happy."

And when he couldn't, she went looking for someone who would.

He gave her a reassuring nod. "I think we can both carry our fair share of the responsibility for a failed marriage. Neither of us had the best upbringing. Good role models. I was no more mature than you were. Didn't have a clue as to how to make a relationship work."

"But I used Joey against you time and time again. And that other business… I'm sorry, Cash. I didn't think you'd end up doing jail time. I just—"

"Wanted to stop me from gaining custody of Joey."

"Not because I was so good for him, but because I wasn't thinking straight. I was involved with a man who was controlling, jealous, sometimes abusive. And when he hit me after he wouldn't believe why you'd come by the apartment…well, he talked me into using that injury against you to prove my loyalty to him." She leaned in close to whisper in his ear. "But you can forget me confessing that in a courtroom, Cash. Not going to happen."

"Too late now anyway. I did the time." He offered a weary smile. "As it turns out, good stuff came of it."

She drew back. *"Good?"*

He nodded. "When you're over here sometime to visit Joey, I'll tell you about it. You might find it changes your life for the better, too."

She looked at him as if he'd grown a second head, but just then he glimpsed Rio moving toward the exit doors. "Just a second, Lorilee. I'll be right back."

He intercepted Rio as the automatic doors slid open.

"You're leaving? Without seeing Joey?"

Not staying to talk further to *him*?

"ICU has restricted visitation. I wouldn't think of shortchanging you or Lorilee. But Grandma Jo called and she and Mom are on their way over—Mom's bringing your truck—and I'm sure they'll want to see the little guy. She said, too, that they'd be more than happy to take Lorilee back to Canyon Springs afterward."

"Joey will probably want to see *you* when he wakes up, though."

"Tell him I'll see him when he gets out of the hospital. That I'll be planning his next riding lesson."

"That may be a while, but I'll tell him. It might give him something to look forward to." He offered a tight smile. "That is, if this episode with Wild Card doesn't put him off horses permanently."

"I'd be surprised if it did. I see too much of his father in him."

He grimaced. "Stubborn you mean? Pigheaded? Lacking in self-control?"

"Actually…" She looked up at him, her expression unexpectedly tender. "I was thinking more along the lines of determined, persevering, faith-filled."

"Into self-delusion these days, are you?"

Her gaze lingered. "Calling them as I see them, cowboy."

And with that, she turned and headed out the door, leaving his heart heavy with what-might-have-beens.

Chapter Sixteen

She'd wasted too much time allowing her past to color her future—to distort her relationship with a man she'd come to love.

And had now lost.

Rio lifted her saddle to the tack room's rack. Straightened the stirrups.

Yes, Cash had struck Eliot with a ferocity that had frightened her. But could she truly fault him for that? It *was* instinctive, in self-defense. He'd been ashamed afterward. Regretted it. Seth had never felt ashamed. The only regret he ever expressed was getting caught for something he shouldn't have been doing in the first place. He'd insisted he wouldn't have hit her if she hadn't "made" him mad.

That wasn't Cash. But in misplaced fear, she'd put him in the same box with Seth, slammed on the lid and tied it shut with a nice neat bow. And in doing so, she'd hurt Cash deeply.

How could she ever make it up to him?

"You're here."

Startled, she turned to see Cash standing in the tack room doorway. He'd been keeping diligent watch at the hospital, and she hadn't seen him for several days. Her only updates on Joey had come from Luke and Delaney, who'd welcomed "Junior"—Kaysen Dean—into the world at the same hospital that week.

"I'm here," she said lightly, not wanting him to know how his unexpected arrival had shaken her. How her heart had grieved for days. "I just got back from a ride. Needed to clear my head."

"I get that. I can hardly wait to get back in the saddle myself." He nodded in the direction of the stalls behind him. "I see Wild Card's gone."

"Brax came and got her the day after the accident." She looked at him uncertainly, not sure how he'd take that. "He felt awful about what happened to Joey."

He reached out to fiddle with a lead rope hooked on the wall. "She'll never be a beginner's horse, but given the time, I think I could still make her a decent mount for an experienced rider. I don't think she's so much mean as there are deep-seated fears that need to be worked out of her."

Like those God was working out of *her*?

"With those issues, though, she doesn't belong where we're hosting guests. She's too much horse for Brax, and he should have sold her months ago." Rio adjusted the bridle on its hook above the saddle. "So how *is* Joey?"

"He's coming home tomorrow."

She met his gaze with a relieved smile. "That's wonderful news, Cash."

"I couldn't be happier. He says he misses Misty and can't wait to see her."

Rio folded her arms, a smile widening. "What did I tell you? Like father, like son."

"You were right." He squinted one eye. "But then you've been right about quite a few things."

And wrong about others.

"You can tell him Rags misses him, too," she said hurriedly. "And that Misty stands over by the fence every morning, waiting for him. Then eventually gives up and wanders off."

"I'll do that." He glanced at his watch. "Lorilee's spending the morning with him, so I thought I'd get the cabin ready for his return. Catch up on some things. Thanks for covering for me while I've been gone. I've been a slacker this week."

She gave him a dubious look. "I hardly think being by your son's side at a time like this would constitute a slacker. I've been more than happy to do whatever I can."

"It's appreciated." He considered her for a long moment. "I can't thank you enough, Rio, for finding Lorilee. Joey was happy to see her, and even confessed he didn't talk about her because he was afraid something had happened to her. Nobody was telling him, and he didn't want to ask and have it confirmed."

Her insides crumpled. "Oh, Cash, that's heartbreaking."

"It is. Clueless me I should have recognized that's what was going on with him. That his grandma hadn't explained anything when she brought him up here. But it's all good now. And totally amazing the way you found his mom, wasn't it?"

"I can't take credit. It was definitely a God thing."

"But you were the instrument He used because He knew you'd be alert and follow through."

She squirmed a little under his grateful gaze.

"Is Lorilee still agreeable with transferring custody to you? She hasn't changed her mind?"

He flashed a relieved smile. "No mind changing.

She insists she's carried the load eight years, and now it's my turn."

"I'd say you've borne a fair share of that load. You've worked hard to provide child support, insurance, to spend as much time with Joey as you could—when his mom allowed."

He chuckled. "Maybe so, but I didn't carry the day-to-day responsibilities, and I now know how much work that is. So if she wants to believe I didn't play a part for eight years, I'm good with that. I'm just grateful she didn't decide to take him back after what happened while he was in my care. I got the impression that some-thing *you* said kept her from going off the deep end on that. From blaming me."

"Or maybe God's been working in her heart."

"Could be."

Cash glanced in both directions down the aisle be-hind him, then to her surprise stepped into the tack room and slid the door closed.

He squared his shoulders, looking her in the eye. "What I actually came to see you about is to apologize for jumping to negative conclusions when you tried to tell me how you'd found Lorilee, and to let you know that Joey and I—"

She held up a restraining hand.

"No, Cash. I owe *you* an apology." She'd so desper-ately hoped and prayed for this opportunity to talk to him. To make things, if not right, at least better. "I al-lowed my experiences with another man to unfairly overshadow my impressions of you."

"You were right to."

"No, I wasn't. I'd wrongly judged you, believed your ex-wife's accusations despite what your friend Will had told Grandma Jo. I'd convinced myself that if a jury found you guilty, you were guilty. Because of my past, I stubbornly—fearfully—refused to accept anything else."

"There was no way to prove the accusations false, though. It was a case of he-said, she-said. And with my track record..."

"You were wronged, Cash. I believe that now. I'd believe it even without Will's confirmation. And I'm sorry for not trusting you."

For pushing you away.

"I appreciate your telling me that." But he sounded resigned. Weary. She was responsible for that, at least in part.

"You're a good man, Cash. A man with a heart for God. A good father to your son."

And you'd make me a wonderful husband.

"You helped me see, too," she continued, "that God didn't bargain with me to spare my mother's life. I admit I struggled with your viewpoint. But I believe now that His plan was to use Mom's situation—my vow—to nurture a too-long ignored dream to make a difference in the world. To help other victims of dating violence. To bring good from a bad experience."

Cash winced. "I'm sorry, Rio, that my behavior that night in Canyon Springs brought it all back. Forced you to relive that fear. And to fear *me*."

"I don't fear you now."

"For which I'm grateful." Their gazes held briefly, his relief genuine. Then he looked away. "So you're going to finish up that degree, right?"

"With my transferable hours from the junior college combined with those from my freshman year, I figure I might have another year and a half, possibly two. For undergrad, anyway."

"Then you plan to work on a university campus after that."

He made that a statement, not a question, based on their earlier conversations.

"Not necessarily." She brushed her hair back. "There's dating—and domestic—violence all around us. People who need guidance, counseling."

"Sad state of affairs this country has gotten itself into. We've done our best to push God out of it, and now we're reaping the rewards."

"We are." She drew a breath. "So I'll get my degree and see where God leads."

Back to Hunter Ridge? To the Arizona mountain country where Cash and Joey would be building a future?

"I wish you all the best." He looked away for a moment, then back at her. "Anyway, as I started to say… Joey and I'll be leaving the Hideaway as soon as I find another job and a managerial replacement can be found for the horse operation."

An invisible fist squeezed the air slowly from her lungs. *He was leaving?*

"I don't know how soon that will be," he continued, "but there's no reason to change your college plans. I'll make sure the season is covered until it wraps up later in the autumn and the horses are shipped south for the winter."

"But I thought…"

That he'd be here forever? That although things hadn't worked out between them, she'd see him when she came home from school on weekends and holidays? That maybe, just maybe, over time God would mend their mutual hurts, lead Cash to forgive her for her hardness of heart and open a door to a shared future?

"I've talked to your Grandma Jo," he went on, "and we've reviewed the applications that came in a few months ago at the time I applied. A few look promising, and maybe some of the applicants are still available. Hopefully, I can get my replacement brought up to speed before this current season's over."

She swallowed the lump in her throat. He'd discussed this with Grandma, and even knowing how her granddaughter felt about him she was going to let him head off into the sunset, never to be heard from again?

"Don't leave, Cash. You're needed here."

"I think it would be best for all concerned if I did."

"I disagree. You're good for the Hideaway."

For me.

He cared for her. She knew he did. But had her apology not done a thing to repair the damage she'd done? Impulsively, she stepped forward and slipped her arms around the startled man's neck.

"You and Joey belong here, Cash. This is your home now. Don't leave."

Don't leave me.

Rio didn't want him to leave. His heart pounding, Cash stared down into her beautiful eyes. Eyes clearly speaking an unmistakable love he'd only dreamed of—and calling him to declare his.

But he couldn't. Nor could he remain at Hunter's Hideaway.

He wasn't the man he'd once naively thought he'd become. He needed more time. Time to grow. Change. To become the kind of man a woman like Riona Hunter deserved.

"We both need to move on." He leaned in to gently kiss her forehead when every ounce of his being screamed to pull her into his arms and beg her to spend the rest of her life with him.

But although she said she trusted him, didn't fear him—words his heart had hungered to hear—he didn't trust himself. Until he could do that, he could offer her nothing. Maybe on down the road. Maybe if she didn't find someone worthy of her while she was in school… but not now.

It would be unfair to give her false hope.

Woodenly removing her arms from around his neck, he stepped back, his hands clasping hers as he gazed tenderly into her eyes. But before he could say anything more, the tack-room door slid open with crash.

"Keep your hands off her, Herrera."

Cash released Rio and turned warily to Eliot Greer whose big body filled the door. But too late he recognized the other man's intent. A monster-size fist slammed into his stomach, doubling him over and sending him crashing into a saddle rack. He went down hard, the wind knocked out of him.

"Eliot!" Rio lunged at the other man.

He grabbed her by the arm and pulled her aside. "Stay out of the way, sweetheart. I've had enough of this guy taking liberties with you that he has no right to take. I've been keeping an eye on him. Didn't think I'd see you slippin' in here, did you, Herrera?"

Cash stared up at him, his voice low. Deadly. "Take your hands off her, Greer, or answer to me."

"I don't think that's your call to make," the other man mocked. "You came back here full of yourself just like your old man, who thought he could lay claim to any woman he set his eyes on. Maybe everyone else is willing to look the other way, but I'm not. So let's settle this once and for all."

Cash's fingers fisted as a familiar inner fire raged through him. This guy needed knocking into the next county, and Cash was more than happy to be the one to do it.

Recognizing Cash's intent, Eliot held out one hand to keep Rio back as his gaze flitted nervously between her and Cash.

"Please, don't do this, Eliot." Desperation colored Rio's voice.

"Stay out of this," Eliot barked. "There's been bad blood between us for a long time. Like father, like son."

"He's nothing like his father. Nothing."

Still prone, as though an invisible hand were holding him down, Cash scowled up at the sneering face. Remembered the day their fathers fought. How he'd laughed and cheered, and how Eliot had glared at him with hate-filled eyes. The same eyes now daring him to meet his challenge.

"Come on, mister, get on your feet and let's get this over with."

Eliot had been ten back then. Proud of his father. Ashamed of his mother. Humiliated that the hated Hodgson Herrera, although ultimately cast out from Hunter's Hideaway, had nevertheless bested Jeb Greer in a fight that even after all these years Eliot hadn't been able to let go of.

Cash again clenched his fists, ignoring the deep ache in his belly. He had no choice but to fight the man. Blood pumping adrenaline through his veins at the unprovoked attack, he wasn't going to let the belligerent man use him for a punching bag. The guy needed to be taught a lesson. And Cash was more than capable of delivering it.

Eliot kicked a curry comb that Cash's fall had jarred

to the floor. It bounced harmlessly off Cash's shoulder. "Come on, get up you coward!"

Having had enough of the big man's bluster, Cash moved to rise again. Then once more halted.

Because you are His son, God sent the Spirit of His Son into your heart...

In his mind's eye, the face of the boy Eliot had once been superimposed itself over that of the hostile hulk standing above him—and an unexpected compassion welled up inside. The child had suffered undeserved humiliation at the hands of a parent's poor choice. Just as Cash had.

Eliot's father had been knocked down by an egotistical man half his size who'd walked away hurling insults as to his opponent's manhood, his inability to keep a wife from running off with a "superior" man. The marriage had shattered. The family unit ripped apart. Only God and Eliot knew how that had eaten away at him through the years.

"Get up, you—" Eliot kicked at him again, this time slamming Cash in the leg. He could have easily grabbed the booted foot and brought the reckless man crashing down, but chose instead to weather the blow.

"Eliot! Stop it!" Rio took a step forward, but the other man blocked her way.

"Looks like you've found yourself a real winner here, Rio. Too spineless to get up on his feet like a man." His lips curling in disgust, he pinned his gaze on Cash. "Nobody would have called your pa *yellow*."

But they'd called his father a lot of other things. Things that, God willing, nobody would ever call the son of Hodgson Herrera.

Who was now a son of God.

He took a weary breath as his own anger drained away. "I'm not going to fight you, Eliot."

"Hear that, Rio? You may want to reconsider the company you've been keeping. Find yourself a *real* man."

"I've found the real man I'm looking for, Eliot." Her determined gaze met Cash's for a startling moment, then again focused on the other man. "And he's not you."

"You're making a mistake, babe."

"No, you made the mistake. You're fired. Go see Luke. Tell him I said you were to pick up your check for this week and next, and get off Hunter property within the hour."

"Are you kidding me?"

"You heard me. And you heard Cash. There's not going to be a fight. And now that you don't have a job, there's nothing to keep you here at the Hideaway. So get out of here. Now."

"You can't—"

"You think not? Then take it up with Grandma Jo— and Deputy Turner if you want me to involve him, too. I'm a witness to an unprovoked assault. A second one, I might remind you. Grandma knows of the first and you were warned, so I'm sure this one will catch her interest."

Eliot's stare of disbelief turned to one of disdain. "I never thought you'd hear me saying this about you, Rio, but you're not thinking straight. You're starting to make me think you deserve this loser. So don't come crying to me."

He gave Cash a scorn-filled look, then strode out the door.

Rio was immediately at Cash's side, but he waved

her away. Easing himself to his feet, the weight that had pressed upon him, forcing him to stay down, now lifted.

In its place an inner assurance had taken hold. As tempting as it had been, as much as the desire had warred within him, he hadn't given in to the other man's relentless baiting.

"You're sure you're okay?"

"Fine." He dusted himself off. He might be in a world of hurt for days from that gut punch, but the elation, the sense of triumph that filled him was already overriding the discomfort. "Thanks for saving me the trouble of firing him."

"Better coming from me than you, I thought. I doubt he'll challenge it with Grandma Jo."

"Or Brax." He smiled. "Although I've on occasion suspected the good deputy would like to deck me himself."

She bent to pick up his hat from where it had fallen, dusted it off and placed it on his head. "You think so?"

"I know so. And if I'm not mistaken, somebody said something to Eliot about having found the man they've been looking for." Cash angled a look at her. "That man have a name?"

"He does."

"Gonna share?"

She tilted her head. "Mmm, that depends on how the man in question feels about the girl in question."

"So…if some guy did this." He tugged her closer, then settled his hands at her waist. "And kissed her like this…"

He lowered his mouth gently to hers. Heard her soft sigh and felt her arms go around his neck as she responded without hesitation.

"Would she then confess his name?" he murmured against her ear.

"That—" her words came somewhat breathlessly "—all depends. There are three missing little words. So it has to be assumed...there are doubts?"

"Assumptions can get you into trouble."

"Maybe. But a girl doesn't want to throw herself at a man uninvited."

He cocked his head, playing along. "So that trio of words would be considered inviting—and might result in her throwing herself at him?"

She pursed her lips thoughtfully, then nodded. "Possibly."

"Well, then..." He gently cupped her sweet face in his hands. "Any doubts I previously harbored had nothing to do with you, Rio. They were all about me."

"But—"

"After that episode at the rodeo, I didn't think I could ever be the kind of man a woman like you could count on. I'd long prided myself on thinking that I'd changed, but that night I discovered the truth. I'd been keeping myself out of temptation's way. Dodging trouble. But I hadn't faced it head-on. I recognized, too, that I had so far yet to go." His gaze searched hers. "But after what happened with Eliot just now..."

"You mean because you didn't punch him clear to the moon?"

A smile tugged at the fact she didn't question that he was capable of doing it.

"That took courage, Cash. An incredible amount of courage."

"It wasn't courage." He shook his head confidently. "That wasn't me who had that kind of self-control, but God's spirit in me. It's evidence that while I'll undoubtedly be tempted again to settle a score with my fists, He's going to be with me. To help me work through those negative feelings and to help me become the kind of man He intends for me to be. The kind of man *you* deserve."

Her expression softened. "I'm not without my own faults. He'll work with both of us."

"He will." Cash clasped his hands around hers, his voice not much above a whisper. "I'm not one for speeches, but I do love you, Rio. With all my heart."

"I don't know exactly when it happened, but as I got to know you, respect you, trust you...saw the way you treasure your son..." She returned his smile. "I love you, too."

Her confession sent off a rumble of fireworks in his heart, nudging him to boldly take that next step. "I know this is rushing things and we'll have to deal with a long-distance courtship for a while, but you have to admit, we do have a fairly lengthy history. So I'm going to ask this right out...will you marry me, Princess?"

He gazed down at her, amazed at the words he'd never dreamed of being given permission to say.

But when she didn't immediately respond, merely stood solemnly staring into his eyes, his throat tightened. Had he gone too far? She wasn't ready for a proposal yet?

Or maybe he shouldn't have called her Princess.

He cleared his throat uncertainly. "Rio, I—"

"You want me to marry you?" Eyes now sparkling, she laughed that beautiful laugh that touched him deep within. "Just try to stop me, cowboy."

Then, pulling her hands free from his, she threw herself into his welcoming arms.

Epilogue

"It's about time the two of you got engaged." Delaney, her baby son in her arms, looked up at Cash with laughter in her eyes. "I thought for a while there that you both were going to blow it."

"Came close. Too close." His gaze drifted across the moonlit patio at the back of the inn where an engagement celebration was well underway. Fairy lights were strung overhead, tables laden with tasty appetizers and a country-western rhythm echoed in the background.

But where had Rio gotten off to?

"As a relative newcomer to this bunch myself," Delaney continued, "welcome to the family. You're going to fit right in."

"There was a time when I was younger that I looked at the Hunter family with all the envy of a kid with his nose pressed up against a candy store window. Not because they owned the Hideaway and all those horses, but because of who they were. How they treated each other. How they put God first in their lives. I sure never dreamed I'd one day be a part of that."

"And it's doubtful you dreamed Rio would grow up

to be such a looker, either," Luke chimed in as he joined his wife and infant.

Cash laughed. "That, too."

"You're a fortunate man, Herrera."

"I don't need reminding of that."

Rio's big brother eyed him. "Treat her right and life—*and I*—will be good to you."

"You can count on it."

He felt a tug at his sleeve and looked down at his son who was managing a plate of goodies amazingly well with only one arm in working order.

"Dad, what's twitterpated?"

"Where'd you hear that word?"

"Uncle Grady says that's what you and Rio are."

Delaney and Luke laughed.

Uncle Grady. Rio was already encouraging Joey to think of her siblings as aunts and uncles, making him feel a part of the family, even though no date had yet been set.

"What's it mean?" Joey persisted.

"Well…" It had been a long time since he'd seen the Disney flick *Bambi*. "Twitterpated is—"

"Twitterpated," Rio joined in from somewhere behind him, and he turned to see her approaching, "means infatuated."

Joey's nose wrinkled. "Fat what?"

"Smitten." She kept a playful gaze on Cash as she closed the distance between them. "Head over heels. Overcome by romantic feelings. Crazy in love."

At which point she stopped directly in front of him and tipped her face up for a kiss—that he obediently delivered.

Joey made a face. "Oh. Mushy stuff."

Still thoroughly amazed that Rio wanted him to be a

part of her life, Cash slipped his arm around her waist. "Yeah, mushy stuff, buddy. Better get used to it."

Joey waved them away with his free hand. "I'm outta here."

No doubt back to the food tables.

Cash chuckled. "Twitterpated. I guess that's what we are, huh?"

"There's no guess about it," Delaney stated. "And people thought Luke and I had it bad."

Rio poked her older brother in the arm. "I can remember when this guy first took notice of you, Delaney. Grady and I teased him mercilessly."

Luke grinned. "You did. Relentless."

"He was such a chicken. Didn't want to admit to anyone that a cute little artist who was in town for the summer might be more than a passing fancy."

"Good reminder, Rio." Delaney peeped around her husband to call out Cash. "You and Rio weren't the only ones who almost blew it. And come to think of it, Grady and Sunshine were a near miss, too. What is it with you Hunters, anyway?"

"Twitterpated," Rio and Cash said together. Then laughed.

The new Hunter infant chose that moment to let out a squall. Delaney looked anxiously at their son, then up at Luke. "Diaper time again?"

"I imagine so."

"Then here you go." She passed the tiny bundle off to her husband before confiding in Rio and Cash. "This is my first. His fourth. So isn't it customary to let those with the most experience do the honors?"

Both nodded agreement, then laughed as the other couple and their now-wailing son moved away to take care of business.

"Cute kid," Cash remarked.

"But ours will be cuter."

"You think so?" He raised a brow. "The first one? Or the second, too?"

"All five."

"Five?" He almost choked. This was the first he was hearing of this.

"Yep, five. Like me and my siblings. Which makes it even more important that I obtain my undergraduate degree ASAP and get myself established in a counseling career. Maybe get my master's going. Then we can get started."

He chuckled, then nudged her. "But if that's a priority, you might also want to work getting married somewhere into your overbooked schedule."

"That, too." Even in the dim light he perceived a blush that accompanied a suddenly shy smile.

He pulled her into his arms. "So, what are you thinking? Next weekend?"

She drew back, her oh-so-kissable mouth open in surprise. "You're kidding, right?"

He shrugged. "I'm good with it."

"Nope. No way. I was actually thinking—"

Please, Lord, don't let her make us wait until she finishes school a year and a half or two years down the road.

It was going to be rough enough this first semester. He'd be burning up the cell phone minutes for sure. Probably tire tread, too.

But if that's what she wanted…

"How about…" From the dancing lights in her eyes, he knew she was enjoying keeping him in suspense. "Christmas Eve?"

His heart soared. While that was a long way off, it

sure beat out a year or two. But what if—? He squinted one eye. "You mean, *this* Christmas, right?"

"No. I mean Christmas when you're forty years old." She gave him a playful rap on the arm. "Of course I mean this Christmas. No way while I'm at school and coming home as many weekends as I can am I going to let you run loose, free and single, for some other woman to get her hands on."

He tugged her closer. "There's no danger of that. I only have eyes for you, Princess."

Her expression softened. "And I for you, cowboy."

"I want this marriage to work, Rio. But I know good marriages like your folks have don't come by accident. We've got to put God first in our lives, even over each other. We need to accept and appreciate each other for who God made us to be."

"Extending forgiveness when needed and looking for ways to bless each other every day."

"I love you, Rio."

"And I love you."

He cut a covert glance around the patio, teeming with guests, but nobody seemed to be paying them any attention at the moment. Tightening his grip on her waist, he gazed down into the eyes of the woman he wanted to spend the rest of his life with. "Looks like the coast is clear. Wanna seal those declarations with a kiss?"

Eyes filled with tenderness, the corners of her lips curved upward. "I insist on it."

She slipped her arms around his neck. And with a grin he dipped her dramatically and settled his mouth on hers—to the resounding hoots, cheers and applause of family and friends who loved them.

* * * * *

Don't miss these other
HEARTS OF HUNTER RIDGE *stories*
from Glynna Kaye:

REKINDLING THE WIDOWER'S HEART
CLAIMING THE SINGLE MOM'S HEART
THE PASTOR'S CHRISTMAS COURTSHIP
THE NANNY BARGAIN

Find more great reads at www.LoveInspired.com

Dear Reader,

Thank you for joining me in Arizona mountain country as Cash and Rio journey on a rocky road to a happily ever after!

Cash had struggled through the betrayal of someone he'd loved. Rio, likewise, learned things about herself and the one she'd given her heart to that left her empty. Both are wounded souls. People who, because of past experiences, question their self-worth and are suspicious of the motives of others. They are people who doubt they deserve love and who desperately need to recognize that the love God offers is not "deserved," not "bargained for," but a free gift because He loves them unconditionally. Don't we all need the kind of love only God can give us through his son Jesus Christ?

If, like Rio, you are in a destructive relationship—or know someone who is—seek help or encourage them to seek it. While I don't have the background, training or connections to personally help you, there are those who do. Churches, campus counselors, law enforcement, community and faith-based shelters. And *never forget* God loves you!

You can contact me at Love Inspired Books, 195 Broadway, 24th Floor, New York, NY 10007. Or via email at glynna@glynnakaye.com. Please stop by loveinspiredauthors.com and Seekerville.blogspot.com—designated as one of *Writer's Digest* magazine's 101 Best Websites for Writers. We love readers, too!

Glynna Kaye

Get 2 Free Books,
Plus 2 Free Gifts—
just for trying the Reader Service!

Love Inspired®

When Erica Lindholm and her twin babies show up at his family farm just before Christmas, Jason Stephanidis can tell she's hiding something. But how can he refuse the young mother, a friend of his sister's, a place to stay during the holidays? He never counted on wanting Erica and the boys to be a more permanent part of his life…

Read on for a sneak peek of
SECRET CHRISTMAS TWINS
by **Lee Tobin McClain,**
part of the **CHRISTMAS TWINS** *miniseries.*

Once both twins were bundled, snug between Papa and Erica, Jason sent the horses trotting forward. The sun was up now, making millions of diamonds on the snow that stretched across the hills far into the distance. He smelled pine, a sharp, resin-laden sweetness.

When he picked up the pace, the sleigh bells jingled.

"Real sleigh bells!" Erica said, and then, as they approached the white covered bridge decorated with a simple wreath for Christmas, she gasped. "This is the most beautiful place I've ever seen."

Jason glanced back, unable to resist watching her fall in love with his home.

Papa was smiling for the first time since he'd learned of Kimmie's death. And as they crossed the bridge and trotted toward the church, converging with other horse-drawn sleighs, Jason felt a sense of rightness.

Mikey started babbling to Teddy, accompanied by gestures and much repetition of his new word. Teddy tilted his head to one side and burst forth with his own stream of nonsense syllables, seeming to ask a question, batting Mikey on the arm. Mikey waved toward the horses and jabbered some more, as if he were explaining something important.

They were such personalities, even as little as they were. Jason couldn't help smiling as he watched them interact.

Once Papa had the reins set and the horses tied up, Jason jumped out of the sleigh, and then turned to help Erica down. She handed him a twin. "Can you hold Mikey?"

He caught a whiff of baby powder and pulled the little one tight against his shoulder. Then he reached out to help Erica, and she took his hand to climb down, Teddy on her hip.

When he held her hand, something electric seemed to travel right to his heart. Involuntarily he squeezed and held on.

She drew in a sharp breath as she looked at him, some mixture of puzzlement and awareness in her eyes.

What was Erica's secret?

And wasn't it curious that, after all these years, there were twins in the farmhouse again?

Don't miss
SECRET CHRISTMAS TWINS
by Lee Tobin McClain, available November 2017
wherever Love Inspired® books and ebooks are sold.

www.LoveInspired.com

LIEXP1017